BLOOD

A KILLER'S LOVE SERIES BOOK FOUR

JENNIFER IVY

Dedication

For those that like their morally grey men a little playful.

TRIGGER WARNINGS

This book is a Dark Romance, and as such may contain subject matters, content, or events that you may find disturbing.

This includes but is not limited to:

Dubious Consent (Dubcon)

Blood

Gore

Taboo relationship between adopted siblings

Car accident

Mention of miscarriage/pregnancy loss

Graphic descriptions of Violence, Torture, and Murder.

BLOOD

A KILLER'S LOVE SERIES BOOK FOUR

JENNIFER IVY

CHAPTER ONE

Kaleb

My chest heaves and my throat burns with every panted breath. Puffs of cold air collect in front of my face as my fingers grapple with my belt buckle.

Outside at the end of October isn't the ideal time for this, but it's been fucking weeks, and I'm done waiting.

I need this.

The knife tucked beneath my tee presses farther into my back with every jostle of the leather in my hands. A sharp reminder of what may come after.

My cock couldn't get any harder.

Leaves crunch as the woman in front of me crawls backward. The lip between her teeth hides her own rushed breaths, but her bare chest is proof of our little chase.

"Don't you fucking dare," I snarl.

Her hands still, clutching the edges of her torn blouse.

"I'm cold." She shivers.

"I don't fucking care."

I'm not paying her to be fucking warm.

She matches my glare with one of her own, her black eyebrows pull down, and the sight annoys me. I glance at her golden locks. *The next one needs to be a natural blond.*

My cock throbs, reminding me of why I'm in the woods in the middle of fucking winter. With my belt open, my fingers move to my zipper.

"Money first!"

Reaching into my back pocket, I pull out my wallet before tossing two hundred dollars onto the frosted ground at her feet. "Tits out and pull up your fucking skirt," I order. The metal at my back shifts again, tempting me to end tonight in more than a quick fuck.

"Asshole," she whispers.

I drop to my knees between her spread legs with a chuckle. "What I'm about to do to you makes me an asshole."

Opening my wallet again, I grab the small wrapper tucked next to the bills at the back and secure it between my teeth, then I drop my wallet beside her hip.

Shuffling forward, I release my pants button and

reach into my boxers, hissing as my cold fingers brush the sensitive skin aching for attention.

"I'm wet and ready."

"I don't care." I shoot back through my clenched teeth.

The tips of my fingers barely wrap around my cock when my text tone pierces the air. Rolling my eyes, I brush it off.

It's probably the family group chat.

But it sounds again and again. Three quick texts followed by silence. *Fuck!* Condom still in my mouth, I keep my eyes on the woman spread out before me as I dig out my cell.

Dad: 911

Dad: 911

Dad: 911

Fuck! Fuck! Fuck!

Everything around me falls away. Spitting the condom wrapper on the ground, I stagger to my feet and press the call button. My chest restricts, and my breaths halt, but it's not the cold. Panic surges through me with every ring that sounds in my ear.

My stomach drops when it goes to voicemail. Ending the call, I try again. And again. Why the fuck is he not answering?

My hands shake as I scroll to my mother's number. She always answers. Always.

"Come on, come on," I plead, turning away from the body still laid out on the ground.

I call my brothers next—Daniel and then Michael.

My vision blurs more and more with every unanswered call. *I can't lose another family.*

Spinning, I startle the woman, causing her to drop back down, but she quickly sits up when I rush over.

Bending down, I snatch my wallet. I press call for Daniel's wife, but Charlie's call goes unanswered too.

"What are you doing?"

I don't bother looking at her. Instead, I wedge my cell between my shoulder and ear, shove my wallet into my back pocket, and refasten my pants.

Walking away, I leave her sitting on the cold soil.

"Hey! Wait! Where the fuck are you going?"

I don't know why I answer, but I do. "Home."

"Was it her?" she asks, scurrying to catch up.

Lara's voicemail sounds in my ear. I don't leave a message. Daniel's wife didn't answer, and neither did Michael's. I blink quickly.

"Who?" I growl, pulling the cell away from my face. *Why is no one in this family answering?* Desperate, I search for Sam's number, Daniel and Michael's sister. Typing in Brat, I send up a silent prayer.

Please answer.

But it's no good. My heart squeezes again. I'm going to have a heart attack at twenty-seven.

The woman beside me wrestles with her shirt, fastening the buttons as she shivers in the cold air. "Sammy," she mutters distractedly.

My whole body freezes—my legs, my heart, my breath.

Seeing my face, she rushes on, "You called me that earlier when you chased me. Figured she was your girlfriend."

"You figured wrong," I sneer through clenched teeth. "Never say that fucking name again," I hiss, my finger near her face.

Seeing her cower, I curse.

Pushing forward on unsteady feet, I fight the direction of my thoughts and why my family isn't answering. But it's no good.

Three 911 texts are something that my brothers and I agreed on as our way of saying life and death. Images of worst-case scenarios assault me while my rig comes into view. I need to get back to Cromwell Town. Now.

If they're gone, then so am I . . . right after I kill every motherfucker involved.

I'm not living this shitty life without them.

My sixth call to Michael goes to voicemail. "Answer the fucking phone!" My roar carries out into the dark night. I glance around the area for any threat, but no one is parked close by.

Not for the first time, I'm grateful to have parked at the back of the truck stop. Something that feels like hope mixes with my fear until I remember that life and death are the only reasons for that text.

Dread settles heavily in my stomach, and saliva fills my mouth.

I'm going to be sick.

Fishing out my keys, I pocket my phone for just a second. Gripping the handle on the side of the truck with one hand and the inner door handle with the other, I heave myself inside. My hand shakes as I reach out to close the door, but a petite blonde blocks it.

"What about me?" she asks incredulously.

"Move!"

"How am I supposed to get back to town?" she huffs.

"You're in a fucking truck stop with dozens of lonely men. I'm sure you'll figure something out." Pulling the door closed, I force her to step out of the way.

She throws up her middle finger, stepping farther back.

Rolling my neck, I start the truck and call my dad again.

I'm not a good person. I don't deserve most things. But over my dead fucking body will I lose this family.

The engine roars as I head toward the lot entrance, the whore giving me a few creative gestures in my side mirror. But she doesn't matter. Nothing does. Nothing but my family.

Four hours.

I'm four hours from home.

I crank up the speed as I merge onto the I-90. Sniffing, I breathe out a stuttered breath.

Four long fucking hours.

CHAPTER TWO

Kaleb

The truck rumbles beneath me as I slow to a stop. The turn to my parents' cabin taunts me from the driver's side mirror. Shifting into reverse, I spin the wheel quickly and release the brake.

I need to get off this road without being seen. It's not easy in a vehicle this big, but I'm a good driver. That's why I get first choice of the big deliveries. My lips tug up when a memory of Christopher Cromwell teaching me how to drive flashes through my mind.

"If you can't do it well, don't do it." It was his motto for our lessons.

After checking my mirrors again, darkness greets me in the lane. *Good.*

Pride and panic flow through me as I maneuver

the truck onto and down the small dirt road. Large trees stretch high on both sides.

Private and quiet. Perfect for our family weekends. And an ambush.

Whoever is responsible has no idea what they're in for.

Every single member of my family had better be okay. Not a hair out of place. But I know what killers do. My fear spikes, and my imagination spirals again.

Flicking the headlights off just before the house comes into view, I slow the truck to a stop.

This is it.

Swallowing hard, I grip my knife handle. My palm is sweating as I climb down from the truck. Shadows engulf me as I run along the edge of the forest. The road suddenly feels twice the usual length until I reach where four cars are parked. Not recognizing the black Ford, I head straight for it. With my body bent over, I remain low, using my parents' and Samantha's cars for cover. Sneaking around to the front, I place my hand on the hood of the Ford . . . cold.

I don't know what I was expecting. It's been almost four hours and two hundred and twelve unanswered calls since I got the 911 text.

The weapon in my hand shakes, and my heart gives another sharp squeeze. If anything has happened to my family, I'm going to gut the people responsible, no matter how many have to die tonight. With any luck, they'll take me with them.

Bile rises in my throat.

The Cromwells taught me what it is to be a family. Helen and Samantha Cromwell taught me how to love and be loved. My brothers showed me what true loyalty looks like, and Dad . . . he proved that fists and fear aren't needed to run a household.

Taking the porch steps two at a time, I hurry to the door. The blade of my knife catches the light streaming through the glass of the front door. Lace covers the small window, blocking my view inside, but heavy footsteps sound out. Someone just walked from the kitchen to the living room, where the front door will open.

Time for quiet and sneaky is gone. My family is in this house. The knife spins in my hand, nerves ruling me. Anyone who gets between me and them fucking dies.

Tossing the knife a hundred and eighty degrees, I catch it in my fist, the back of my hand closer to the blade.

With one last deep breath, I turn off my brain and get ready to react on instinct. I clench my right fist tightly, and with a flick of my left hand, I shove the front door open.

CHAPTER THREE

Samantha

"Baby, go to bed."

Blinking sleepily, I smile over at my mom. "I'm okay," I whisper, tugging my blanket higher.

"You can hardly keep your eyes open, Sammy." She tuts from the chair next to my sofa.

I smile at the nickname. My family rarely uses it. "I know, but Kaleb will be here soon, and I want to be down here when he gets here."

"He never texted me back, sweetheart. He was probably already sleeping and won't see it until he wakes later," my dad adds from the kitchen.

"He'll be here. Pauline said if he was on schedule, he should have been parked up and around four hours away from home, remember? He'll be here," I repeat. "Besides, I don't want to leave Shelby on her own." I nod at my best friend curled up on the sofa opposite the one I'm stretched out on.

"She's hardly alone, baby. Your mom and I will be down here, and we're definitely not sleeping." Dad chuckles, walking into the living room and over to my mom. Joining her, he sits on the arm of her chair, passing her a bowl of chopped strawberries. "My love." He smiles down at her, and it makes me melt.

I want that. I want a man to look at me like I'm his whole world. Glancing down at my watch, I check the time again.

"Mom?"

I chuckle at Michael's voice floating out of the cell on my mom's quilt-covered lap. The sound of voices and movement coming from the phone has become a part of our night, with my mom and Michael refusing to end the call.

"Oh shoot." Mom jumps, grappling to pick up the phone. "How's Charlie? Any progress? How's the baby?" she rushes, bombarding my older brother with questions.

His deep sigh rings out over the loudspeaker. "The baby's heart rate has dropped a bit more. They're getting Charlie ready for a C-section now. We're heading down in a minute."

"We? They're letting you go in with Daniel?" Dad asks.

"Err, yeah." Without seeing him, I know Michael is cringing.

"Let's just say after the panic attack Daniel had when the heart monitor started beeping loudly, the hospital staff isn't willing to separate him and Michael anytime soon," my brother's wife, Lara, explains.

"Daniel freaked out, and Michael calmed him down?" my mom asks.

"Yes, ma'am," Lara confirms.

"And then, you calmed Michael?"

The sound of a kiss comes out of the phone before Michael confirms, "She always calms me." We hear him kissing his wife again.

"Gross," I call out, earning a chuckle from everyone on the call.

"I'm going to tell Kaleb not to give you any sugar while you're with him," Michael taunts me.

"Oh please, like I need that man's permission. I'm a grown woman. In fact, he does as I tell him," I lie.

Michael's laughter is loud and contagious, and everyone else joins in.

Rolling my eyes, I huff a chuckle. "Whatever."

"Have you explained to Charlie and Daniel why your dad and I aren't there yet?"

"It's fine, Mom. They understand. Given what's been happening in town lately, they wouldn't have it any other way," Michael reassures her.

"I know, I know. I'm just worried and really want to be there. How's Belle?"

"Asleep," Lara says. "The little lady has been happy to hang with me in the waiting room. We colored our hearts out until she fell asleep."

"You're only an hour and a half away, so as soon as Kaleb gets here, your dad and I will be on our way. We'll get a couple of hotel rooms before coming to get Belle," Mom relays the plan.

"And by that, she means I'll watch Belle while she frets over Charlie and the new baby," Dad corrects.

"Sounds like a plan." Michael makes a sound of confusion. "I'm surprised Kaleb hasn't contacted you yet. Protocol is to call. He should have at least text to confirm he's on his way."

"Maybe he was asleep," Dad defends.

"Doesn't matter," Michael disagrees. "He should have responded anyway. Are you sure he hasn't called?"

Mom, Dad, and I look between us for a second before Mom shrugs.

"It wouldn't matter if he called me. I have all numbers on Do Not Disturb so that this call wasn't affected."

Dad settles his hand on her shoulder. "My phone hasn't rung."

"Are you sure?" Michael asks.

"Pretty sure," he mumbles, but he's already up and moving.

"I don't even know where my phone is." I shrug.

Michael sighs. "You need to stop doing that. What happens if you have an emergency?"

"I'm always with one of you. What kind of emergency am I going to have?" I argue.

"Oops." Dad walks back into the living room, his phone held high and the screen black. "It died," he confirms as he crosses behind the sofa where Shelby is sleeping.

"Oh fuck!" Michael curses through the phone.

CHAPTER FOUR

Kaleb

The front door swings open, and bright lights from the living room blind me for a second, but I don't wait for my eyes to adjust. Instead, I just react.

Lunging forward through the entryway, I grab the man standing behind the sofa. His back hits my chest as I wrap my arm around his neck. I have him in a chokehold before he can even react.

Our bodies have a similar build, and he's a little over six feet. We're evenly matched on size, but I'm younger and running on pure adrenaline.

Screams ring out, piercing the quiet night. The blade of my knife touches his neck at the same time a woman shoots up into a sitting position on the sofa, her scream joining the others.

"Kaleb! Kaleb!" several voices scream, but only one stands out.

Blinking, I look around for my brother. The circles of light slowly leave my vision, giving me a clear image of my mother's terrified face. My head snaps to the left. Dad! *Shit.*

Immediately releasing him, I step back, the knife dropping from my hand as if it burned me. Silently, it hits the rug.

"Fuck, I'm sorry," I rush, watching my dad raise a trembling hand to his neck.

"Jesus Christ, son." His voice shakes.

"Is anyone here?" I ask, looking around. "Were you attacked?"

Shelby drops back down, her hands clutching her chest as she lies there. Mom covers her face, her shoulders shaking.

"Are you okay?" I ask, looking between them until I settle on Samantha.

"No, dickhead. I just lost ten years. What's the matter with you?" she demands, throwing her arms up. "Shelbs, you okay?"

A trembling hand pops up high enough for me to see it over the back of the sofa. A thumbs-up. "Lost a few years too, but I'm good."

At least one of us is good.

I turn to my sister and ask, "What's the matter with me?" I raise my voice. "What's the matter with you?" I turn my attention to Dad. "You text me 911, and then no one answers their cell?"

"Is anyone injured?" Michael asks.

I look around for him again.

"He's not here." Dad huffs, walking away to comfort my mother. "He's on the damn phone." The cell lands with a thud as he tosses it onto the coffee table.

I take a deep breath and close my eyes. "If no one has been attacked or dying, why did you send me a 911?" I try to calm down, but my voice still quivers.

"Attacked or dying?" Dad asks, confused.

"That's what 911 means," I stress, throwing out my arm.

"Shit," Michael spits. "Dad, tell me you didn't just text him 911?" When no answer comes, Michael continues, "Oh my God, tell me you didn't do something crazy to get home."

My body sags as my adrenaline starts to wane. Reaching out, I hold the back of the sofa where Shelby lies. Opening my eyes, I huff a laugh when I see her cute round face smiling up at me.

"Broke a few speeding laws, might get a couple of tickets. Oh, and I almost slit our dad's throat when I thought he was some madman holding my family hostage," I say nonchalantly.

"Dad, are you okay?" Michael rushes.

"Fine, I'm fine. Got a few years scared out of me too, but I'm fine. Sorry, kiddo," he adds, looking over at me. "In my defense, your brother told me to text you 911. That you'd know what it meant."

I laugh. "It means life and death. To get home now."

"Michael!" Dad admonishes. "He forgot to mention that." He huffs, giving me a guilty look.

I breathe out a laugh. "You nearly gave me a heart attack, and I nearly murdered you. How about we call it even?"

He stares at me for a minute before shaking his head. "We're not even."

I watch as he pushes up off the armrest, and before I know it, he has me wrapped in a bear hug.

"What's this for?" I whisper.

"For coming in here like you're John Wayne trying to save this family." Dad pulls back just enough to see my face, his hand wrapped around the nape of my neck. "Not many men would. I owe you for that."

I blink quickly. "Anytime," I promise.

"What's happening?" Michael whispers.

"Dad and Kaleb are hugging. It's gross," Sam answers, earning a disapproving look from Mom.

"Didn't John Wayne use guns?" Shelby asks. "If he came in like John Wayne, he'd have had guns," she states confidently, nodding.

"More like John Wayne Gacy," Sam quips.

"Hey!" Mom, Dad, and Michael admonish.

"That monster did more than kill people. That's not funny, Samantha. Apologize to your brother. Now!" Mom demands.

Stunned silence fills the room. A Helen Cromwell

outburst never happens because the woman is a saint. Literally, she puts up with my brothers and me.

"I'm sorry," Samantha whispers, her eyes focused on me. "Really. It was a joke. You're not an animal."

She means it; I can tell. I give her a small smile to let her know we're okay. If only she knew how many people I've killed over the years.

"You do eat like one, though." She smirks.

There's my girl.

"Samantha!" Dad admonishes again.

Grinning, I wink.

"As long as I don't look like one."

"Nuh-uh." Shelby shakes her head. "Too handsome."

"Thank you, Shelby," I say sweetly, turning to her.

She shrugs nonchalantly. "It's true."

"He knows."

I grin at Sam's dry tone and raise my hand over the sofa for a high five from Shelby, my gaze never leaving Samantha, not until I feel cotton on my palm.

What the fuck?

A laugh bursts out of me, taking the last of my unease when I look down to see Shelby has lifted her foot to high-five my hand.

"I'm not sitting up." She shrugs.

I wrap my hand around her foot before she can pull back and give it a little shake.

"So what was this nonemergency, emergency?" I ask, turning to my dad with a raised brow.

"I need you to watch your sister and Shelby for a few days."

My brows pull into a deep frown. "Last I checked, Samantha was a grown woman." I make a big deal of looking over at her. "Yep, still grown."

My mom tuts and then stands before making her way to three duffel bags sitting by the stairs.

"Is there a threat I don't know about?" I ask my dad. Before he can answer, I look back at Samantha. "Are you okay?"

Sam nods, saying nothing. That alone sets an internal alarm off.

What the fuck am I missing?

"There have been a few burglaries in town over the past week," Dad mutters distractedly as he takes six Tupperware containers and puts them into a cooler bag while Mom goes back to the fridge for more.

"Okay," I sigh, stretching out the word.

"So I need you to babysit," he says like it's obvious.

"And where the fuck are you going?"

"Kaleb!" I close my eyes at my mother's admonishment and pinch the bridge of my nose. I open my mouth but quickly close it.

I need another minute.

By the time I open my eyes, I'm leaning on the back of the sofa again. Samantha smirks at me. She's witnessed me praying for patience enough times that she recognizes the look on my face. I raise a brow.

You can chip in at any time.

Her smirk turns to a toothy smile while she gives me a cute shrug.

I pout my lips to stop my own smile. One deep breath, two. By the fourth, my body starts to relax.

"Of course, I will babysit Samantha and Shelby," I state, stressing the word babysit. Seeing Sam's smile drop makes my own lips tip up. There's no fighting it. My smile wins. Seeing that scowl makes me happy . . . and hard.

Clearing my throat, I push off the sofa. "But why do I need to?"

"Because there's a robber in town, and we can't leave the girls alone to defend themselves. Not that anything is going to happen," he rushes to add.

"I know . . ." I take another deep breath. "Mother!" I call into the kitchen. "Where are you and Dad going?"

"To Charlie," she pants, rushing back to my dad for the fourth time.

How much food are they packing?

Her words take a minute to register. *Charlie?* Why would they rush to see my sister-in-law in the middle of the night?

Surprise covers my face.

"The baby?" I ask excitedly.

"The baby," Mom beams.

My excitement quickly drops. "911."

"No, no," Dad rushes, holding his hand out toward me as if he can stop my racing heart.

"Charlie was feeling lower back pain, more than normal, so she went in for a checkup, and they wanted her to go straight to the hospital. The baby is okay so far, but they need to deliver soon, so she's being prepped for a C-section. Michael and I were watching Belle, so we met them at the hospital. Your mom and dad are coming to help with Belle and to meet the baby." Lara's voice comes through the phone.

Finally, someone who will tell me what's happening. But where's her husband?

"Where's Michael?" I ask aloud.

"He's gone down into surgery. I tell you, Charlie is a better woman than me. Letting her husband's brother be so involved . . . there's no way Daniel will be there when I give birth."

My mom sucks in a loud breath, her head whipping around to look at where the cell sits on the coffee table.

Lara must have heard Mom's gasp. "Later, in the future, many, many years in the future. Definitely not right now."

My heart squeezes at her words. I know how much Michael wants a baby. The sooner, the better, but his wife's wants and needs come first. When she's ready, they'll make it happen.

"Why did you take Belle with you?"

"I panicked." She chuckles. "Michael was . . . well, I don't want to use the word hysterical, but . . ."

Our chuckles mix with hers.

"I couldn't let him drive like that, and it was just safer all around if I came too. Michael wasn't waiting long enough to do a drop-off, so baby girl came with us, and we've been chilling ever since."

"Well, we're packed up and ready to go. We'll be with you soon, baby," Mom tells Lara.

"Great. Do you want to end the call?" Lara asks.

"No, no," Mom rushes before pausing. "Unless you want to?"

"No, no." I can hear Lara smile. "How about you guys play some music in the car ride, though, to keep me awake?"

"Of course!" Mom promises.

"I think we have one of Belle's CDs in the car," Dad adds.

Sam and I manage to smother our laughs, but Shelby's giggle rings out loud and clear.

"What?" he asks, clueless.

"Nothing." The young woman shrugs. "I'm sure nursery rhymes are exactly what she needs to keep her awake."

Mom's hand soothes Dad's shoulder. "I think we can do better than that." She laughs. "Don't worry, sweetheart. We'll keep you wide awake. And if the music fails, I'll just talk to you."

"You want help?" I ask Dad, seeing him start to pick up the bags.

"Yes, please." He smiles gratefully when I take what he's already holding and juggle the other bags until only one small cooler bag is left for him to grab.

I did try to kill the man not too long ago. The least I can do is get the bags.

"Good boy," he praises, which just sets off another round of giggles. Only this time, all of the women are laughing.

"You're all just jealous," I call out, tipping my nose in the air. I keep my expression straight and turn for the door.

Dad's chuckle joins the girls'.

"Let me get the door," he insists, clapping his hand down on my left shoulder.

I raise my brows and lift the bags slightly. "I mean, it's the least you can do."

His grin matches mine.

Together, we make our way to my parents' car, the stillness of the night contagious as silence falls between us. Even the thick wooden steps refuse to creak as we descend them. My dad seems to be lost in thought as he unlocks the car. I turn left to right, checking our surroundings as we step farther from the cabin. The rustling of huge trees in the slight breeze puts me back on edge.

Cromwell is a safe town. A go anywhere, anytime kind of place. It helps that my brothers and I are the only true danger in town, but these break-ins have everyone on edge.

"Kaleb," Dad says, grabbing my attention when I reach the open trunk. Stopping next to him, I load the bags into the car. "I know you think Sam is a grown woman, but this whole breaking and entering has been happening all over town . . ."

"I'll take care of her, Dad. No one gets to her without going through me."

He sighs. "Well, after that display, I can't really worry. Can I?" he asks, nodding at the house.

"The only danger to Samantha is my palm when she no doubt gets bratty and develops an attitude because she's hungry."

His loud laughter slices through the darkness. "You have to stop threatening that. One day, she'll believe you."

My laughter joins his. If only he knew how often his daughter has sported a red ass. My palm twitches just thinking about it. Our parents won't amend her behavior . . . so I do.

My cock twitches at the thought. Feeling excitement hum through my body, I give myself a mental head slap. *She's your sister,* I remind myself. *Is she, though?*

Memories of my childhood before the Cromwells assault me. Hunger, pain, and loneliness. Things a child should never feel, not from their mother. Not that the whore was much of a mother.

My years before joining the Cromwells were full of days sitting outside a small filthy apartment while my mother fucked whichever John had darkened our door.

Helen and Christopher taught me what family is, how to love, how to live.

The whore taught me how to fear, how to hate.

It's because of her I learned how to kill.

It's because of her that I enjoy it.

The Cromwells were too late. They fixed a lot, but there was no repairing that part of me. Images of dead hookers make my pants tight. Reaching down, I discreetly squeeze my crotch as I follow my dad and re-enter the house. Now is not the time.

Frustration joins my arousal. I didn't get the release I needed tonight, a fuck or a kill.

My sigh causes Christopher to turn.

"We're only a call away. An hour and thirty minutes tops. Any issues, just call."

"I'm not worried," I reassure, "just tired. And everything here will be fine. So far, only commercial properties have been burglarized. What are the chances the first home they hit is mine? Update me about Charlie and the baby?"

"Of course, of course."

"Alright, babies, we're leaving," Mom announces. "Girls, behave for Kaleb. Samantha, I'm talking to you." She gives the woman in question a pointed look.

Sam holds her hands out, palms up. "What have I ever done?"

"For starters, we're going to chat about you never answering your phone." I huff.

"I don't know where it is." She shrugs.

"And that's what we'll follow up with."

Sam rolls her eyes. "Daddy, can I please come with you?"

"No."

At her pout, I see him hesitate. So does our mother.

"Sorry, baby, not this time. Your dad and I will be busy helping with Belle, going back and forth from the hospital and the hotel room. People will be sleeping, so there won't be much to do. Besides, you don't want to leave Shelby here by herself, do you?" Mom asks.

"No," Sam mumbles, squinting her eyes at me. "Can you at least tell Kaleb to get the stick out of his ass?"

My face drops to a blank stare. "Is that how we're starting tonight?"

"No," she mumbles again, her eyes flitting from me to my father and back. We both know why. If we had been alone, she'd have added a "sir." I don't push, though. I think we've all had enough tonight.

"I started my night with a heart attack," Shelby chimes in to save her friend. "I'm still having palpitations," she declares dramatically, holding a hand to her chest.

"I think a few hours of sleep will fix that," I tell her, looking down at my watch.

"You ladies grab your bags, please."

"Can't we just stay here?" Sam asks.

"No." I shake my head. When she opens her mouth to speak, I continue, "Baby girl, I'm tired. I have at least three gray hairs now. I want food and to sleep in my own bed."

"Okay," she whispers, losing all her fight. Dragging the blanket off, she rises from the sofa. Shelby follows suit.

I feel even more of my earlier stress melt away when the girls pick up a backpack each from behind Sam's sofa.

"We weren't sure where you wanted to go, so we had them get ready just in case." Mom smiles.

"Thank you," I mouth as we head out and lock up.

"Kaleb, where's your car?" Mom asks, looking around.

I point up the road. "Blocking the exit, so we need to get going, girls." I try to rush them as Mom pulls them in for another hug.

"Oh, hush you." Mom smiles. "We could be gone for a few days. I want to hug my babies one more time." Her arm shoots out in invitation for me to join.

Sighing, I give in because no one tells Helen Cromwell no. Spreading my arms wide, I pull my dad into the hug too and pull my parents close. The five of us stand in a huddle for a few minutes before a final goodbye.

"I love you," I tell them as they climb into my dad's car.

Mom pauses. "We love you too, sweet boy."

"I'm so tired." Sam yawns. "Why did you park so far away?"

"Because I thought someone was murdering my whole family, and I didn't want him to hear me coming when I avenged you," I reply, too tired to filter my response.

Shelby makes a weird gurgle sound, causing me to look. Her hands are clenched into fists as she tries to stop shivering. If her jaw clenches any harder, she'll chip a tooth.

"You should both have coats on. The truck's unlocked, run and climb in." The words are barely out of my mouth before Shelby takes off, making me smile. "Are you not cold?" I ask Sam, who is still walking calmly next to me.

"When have you known me to run?" She frowns. "Unless someone is chasing me, I'm good."

The image warms my body. Being surrounded by tall, thick trees still covering the ground in darkness does nothing to help. Instead, the scenarios keep coming, images of what can never be.

We catch up to Shelby quickly, and she's struggling to pull the door open. "Come here." I place a hand on her back as she steps down and move her to the side slightly before pulling the heavy door open. "Careful," I warn, helping both girls in.

Headlights settle on me as our parents wait for me to move the large truck. Giving a final wave, I climb in behind Sam, discreetly adjusting my cock as I sit. The fucker hasn't gone down since Samantha mentioned being chased.

"This is a really big truck," Shelby comments from the passenger seat, holding her hands over the heating vent even though the truck isn't running. "Do you get lonely driving around all the time?"

With a flick of my wrist, the vehicle rumbles to life.

"No." I smile with a shake of my head. *Company isn't hard to find,* I silently add. Even if they're not the woman I want.

"I wish you wouldn't travel so much," Sam murmurs. Propping her elbows on the two seats, she leans forward from where she is sitting on the small cot that I bed down on while on long hauls.

"I have to work." I shrug.

"I know, but you could work in town or close like Michael and Daniel do."

"Sam," I sigh. We've had this conversation before. She doesn't understand. She never will because I will never tell her the reason I travel—the access it gives me. But we're not doing this tonight. I'm tired, she's tired, and that never ends well.

Sam's arm shoots out as we come to the end of the road, causing me to yank my head back.

"Oh look, you hit the tree. Mustn't have seen it in the dark." She tuts, shaking her head.

My irritation level skyrockets. *She did not just say that?*

"First of all, get your arm out of my face," I start, then tap her arm with two fingers. "Second, I have never, ever hit anything with any vehicle. Never. And third," I snap, turning to her with raised brows, "that" —I point at the deformed tree—"is still a sore subject.

You stole my car and then totaled it by hitting a fucking tree."

"I don't know. That damage looks kind of new." The playful look on her pretty face does nothing to sway my irritation. It was a great car.

"That damage is a year old, and you know it," I tell her, holding up a finger.

Shelby's soft giggle slices the tension.

"Shelly belly, I suggest you remember whose house you will be staying in."

She clears her throat, and I peek over as she forces a serious expression. "That's horrible, Samantha. You should be ashamed, and your license should be cut up."

My lips twitch at hearing my own words from a year ago echoed. Clearly, my girl has been talking.

"You ever gonna get over it?" Sam whispers, leaning closer.

"No."

I loved that fucking car.

"You still love me?"

I don't answer, too busy concentrating on maneuvering the large vehicle out onto the main road. My heart jumps when Sam rests her chin on my shoulder.

Once we're safely out and on our way, I give in. "You know I do, you little brat." Lifting my right hand, I cradle her head and press a kiss to her temple while keeping my eyes on the road.

CHAPTER FIVE

Kaleb

The offices at the truck headquarters are a welcome sight. If I'm not out on the road, I'm working here.

"Can we wait in your car?" Sam asks as we walk into the main building.

"If you want, but it's probably going to be warmer in here," I warn as I wave to Pauline, our overnight manager.

Why didn't I think of her earlier when I was rushing home? Or call the sheriff? *Because I wanted to kill those responsible.*

Being back in the office reminds me that a good release isn't the only thing I didn't get to do while out of town.

"I need to make a call. Go annoy Pauline."

"I prefer to annoy you," Sam sasses, giving me a mischievous smile.

"I know," I tell her, knocking under her chin.

Little shit. My little shit.

We share a smirk, but after a few minutes, Sam spins on the spot and does as she was told, dragging Shelby with her.

I watch as they disappear into the office across from me before slipping into mine. The minute the door is closed, my smile drops.

The whore in the woods had been my plan for tonight, but I had somewhere to go before coming home.

Digging my cell out of the pocket of my pants, I cringe. I'm already not in the mood for this asshole. Watching through the internal window, I see the girls perch themselves on Pauline's desk. The older woman points at the radio system we use to communicate with our drivers and says something. Both their faces light up. You'd think they were twelve, not twenty-two and twenty-three.

The sight relaxes me, and I make the call. He picks up on the fourth ring.

"This is Dr. Brown."

"It's Kaleb Cromwell."

"Oh."

I hear shuffling and a door close before he talks again.

"Why are you calling me?" he spits. "If anyone finds out, I could lose my license."

So fucking dramatic. I roll my eyes.

"Have you got something for me or not?" I ask.

"Depends. What do you have for me?"

Greedy bastard.

I close my eyes and take a deep breath. "I'm not in the fucking mood for you. I had a family emergency. I can't come to your office this month."

The prick huffs, and I can just imagine the horror on his face right now. His cash cow isn't coming to town.

"What do you mean you're not coming to my office this month?"

"What part of that sentence needs to be explained?" I snap.

The line goes dead. He did not!

Motherfucking . . .

This time, he picks up on the first ring, but I don't give him the chance to speak.

"Do that again, and I will put you in your own fucking morgue."

I hear him fumble for words.

"I-I-I just wanted you to realize that I'm serious. I need that money. My girlfriend's pregnant again."

I'm sure his wife is happy about that. This man disgusts me. *Means to an end, Kaleb, you need him,* I remind myself.

"I'll pay double next month," I offer.

"I need it now," he whines.

I open my mouth to ask why he can't wait—the baby isn't going anywhere—but stop myself. I don't care. Not about him, not about whatever fucking issues he's having. What I care about is the information he has.

"So I'll pay by card."

"How do I explain that?"

"I don't fucking care."

Shelby sits in a chair next to Pauline, and they start doing paperwork together.

Maybe she needs a job. I make a mental note to check her finances again since it's been a while. My family and I made sure she was okay after her father passed earlier this year, but she's not been around the house as much since her stepmom moved out of town.

Losing one parent is hard, but two . . .

Pain fills my chest at the thought of losing Helen or Christopher. My eyes search for Sam.

"If you don't have any money, I don't have any information," Brown says. His voice shakes, but there's an undertone to it. He means it.

Shit!

My gaze finds the two women filling out forms.

"Bill me as a patient," I suggest.

"What!"

"You're a doctor, aren't you? Bill me for a consultation or medication." I shrug.

"I'm a coroner," he replies dryly.

"Who also works as the town's only doctor. It's either that or you don't get your money."

A minute of silence stretches between us. This

dick really thinks I didn't check him out before approaching him three months ago.

"I don't like it," he finally adds.

And I don't like you. The previous coroner had been honorable, a good man. His replacement, not so much. This one has a gambling addiction and morals for sale. I'm stuck with him for now. Once I find her, he might just go missing.

"And I don't like paying ten thousand a month, yet here we are. Now, have you found anything?"

"I'll have to charge more than normal, taxes and stuff," he mumbles, still negotiating, but I'm done.

"I don't care. Charge what you want. Did you find her?"

Sam fills my vision, waving at me through the office windows. My throat feels thick. Two women who I'm obsessed with and neither one that I can have.

The woman who birthed me and the woman I live for, my sister. Adopted or not, that's what she is.

But I'm not adopted, am I? My birth mother hadn't cared enough to find me after I ran from her pimp. And even with all the money and resources the Cromwells have, they've never been able to find her.

Didn't help she would leave the game for whatever man wanted her, uprooting us from home to home, never staying for more than a year or two. If we were lucky.

And then there's the fact that she might already be dead.

Blinking, I turn away from Sam.

Helen and Christopher took in an angry, scared boy and showed me love. My brothers showed me how to be at peace with who I am.

"No," Brown says. "The states had thousands of Jane Does in the past ten years alone. I've only managed to check records going back a few years, but none of them match your description."

"She'll be different now."

"I know, I know. I checked. I even widened the scope you gave me. No females between forty and fifty, which is what she'd be now. Well, one came into the hospital the week before last, but it wasn't her."

I'm actually going to kill him.

"Did you go look at her?"

"No!" he screeches. "You can't just go around looking at dead people in other morgues. Not even in my job. I looked at the pictures on their system. I used to work there, and they never revoked my access."

I know. It was the second reason I picked him. He can look at places others can't.

"She was O negative. You said the woman who you're looking for was AB positive. Right?"

"Yes."

A memory of my mother being beaten by a John when I was seven assaults me. It had been bad, worse than usual. We'd had to go to the emergency room, and a sweet lady had let me sit at the nurses' station and color. She'd complimented my neat coloring and steady hand; said I'd make a good doctor.

I smirk. She wasn't wrong. I am good with knives and have even used a scalpel a few times. I'd seen my mother's chart, colored on it. She was AB positive.

"Well, she can't change that. It wasn't her." He pauses briefly before asking, "What billing info do you want to use?"

I roll my eyes and catch sight of Sam and Shelby heading this way. Great, now both of them are bored.

I reel off my home address and reach for my wallet. Flipping it open the same time Sam nudges the office door open just enough to poke her head in.

"Are you done?" she whispers.

I shake my head.

She pouts. "We're hungry."

"Hungry." Shelby nods, her head appearing beneath Sam's.

I raise a brow and point at Samantha. She knows what she's doing. I hate people being hungry. Anyone. When you spend the first half of your childhood begging to be fed, it stays with you.

I never go hungry, and no one I love will either.

"We want waffles," Sam says, but it sounds more like a question.

Shelby nods below her.

Is she kneeling on the floor? The thought makes me chuckle.

"Waffles," Shelby sings.

Sam quickly joins in, "Waffles," pushing the door farther open. She wiggles her arms like noodles and shakes her hips. She looks like a tube man.

Shelby laughs, and before I know it, I have two grown women dancing for waffles in my office doorway.

I hold up two fingers and mouth, "Two minutes." But my smile softens the blow. They slowly back away, wiggling and whisper-singing waffles. Sam holds two fingers up and mouths back, "Two minutes," as she closes the door.

I glance down to grab a card.

What the fuck?

An empty wallet stares back. *Fucking cunt!* I threw my wallet down beside the blonde before I tried to call my dad. *Bitch!* She took everything—cash and cards. The only thing in there is my driver's license.

"Are you there?" the doctor asks.

"Yeah, one second."

I riffle through my desk drawers until I find what I'm looking for. Bingo! Snapping the card up, I breathe a sigh of relief. "Change of address."

I rattle off the company address and card details.

"Pleasure doing business with you. I'll see you next month. Cash."

I don't reply. Instead, I give him a mental middle finger and hang up.

Heading out, I shoot a text to our accountant and ask him to cancel all of my cards and get me replacements ASAP.

Hurrying to the front door, I wave to Pauline. Time to feed my baby and her BFF.

I catch up to them quickly, squeezing my way between them. Once in front, I reenact their dance from in front of my office.

"Waffles, waffles, waffles," I chant, waving my arms and sashaying my hips.

"I feel like we should be paying for this show." Sam's laughter gets louder when I wiggle more.

Rounding to the driver's side, I unlock my car. "Banana and toffee," I state, pointing at Sam. "Banana, toffee, and pecan," I say, pointing at Shelby.

Buckling up, I call my favorite café through the car.

"Judy's café, how can I help?"

"How's my favorite girl?" My smile beams at the giggle that greets me.

"Better now that my favorite boy has called," Judy sweet-talks me. The woman is probably close to eighty and still works her ass off.

"I'm going to tell your husband you said that," I tease.

"Oh hush. He already knows. He's my favorite man, and that's all he cares about."

Sam scrunches her nose. But I think it's sweet. Even in their golden years, Judy and Duke are inseparable.

"I thought you were away driving for a few more days?"

"I was, but Charlie went into labor, so I'm needed for Sam and Shelby," I explain.

"Ahh, say no more."

Like the rest of the town, Judy knows how close our family is.

"What would my favorite customer like?"

I repeat the girls' orders and then add on my own. "Strawberry waffles."

"Extra strawberries, extra waffles," Judy finishes for me.

"I'm feeling extra cream today too, please," I add.

"Ohh." Shelby sits forward in the back seat. "Can I have extra cream too, please?"

I raise a brow and point a finger at Sam, who shakes her head.

"Extra on the pecan one, please, Judy, for takeout."

"You're not coming in?" Judy asks, her voice tinged in disappointment. We do love to have a good gossip session when I'm back in town.

"Not today. It's been a long night, and I need food and sleep."

And a good fuck. But two out of three isn't bad.

"Well, you head on around back, and I'll bring it to you. No wait for you."

"We'll see you soon," I say, ending the call.

Chants of, "Waffles, waffles, waffles," fill the car as I take us across town. Clearly, we're all desperate for sleep.

When we get there, Judy is waiting out back as promised.

Sam and Shelby stay in the car where it's warm while I jump out to get our food.

Holding my arms out, I wrap Judy up in a solid hug. She's the grandmother I never had.

"I hope you're being careful with the burglaries happening."

"Duke's inside. Refused to let me come to work alone like I'm some kind of child. I'd like to see someone try to rob me."

"I wouldn't," I whisper, pulling her in tighter. "Call me if you need me?"

Judy nods, patting my back. "You're a good boy. I'd have had to bribe Junior to watch his sisters."

"How do you know I wasn't bribed?" I ask, pulling back.

Her palm is soft against my cheek. "Because I know you."

Smiling, I raise my shoulders and give a sheepish look. "I'm not so good. I'm having a cash issue, and I'm out until I get new cards. Put it on my tab?" I plead, nodding down at the food bag.

"Tab?" she practically shrieks. "Kaleb Cromwell, you get to eat here for free. We're here because of you," she declares, waving her arm to show the building.

"You're here because you're the best cook in town. I just financed it. Selling out of Duke's gas station just wasn't doing it for me. I needed better access to your food. All day, every day. I may have helped you start, but you keep it alive."

"Well, it still stands."

"I'll pay for it next time," I promise, dropping a kiss on her left cheek. "Besides," I call out on my way back to the car, "the amount I eat here, I'm your profit margin."

Judy laughs, waving to the girls as we pull out and head home. Finally.

CHAPTER SIX

Samantha

Stretching out my legs, I wiggle my toes under the blanket.

Kaleb side-eyes me but ignores my feet.

I glance over at Shelby slouched on the other sofa. Cocooned in her blanket, she can barely keep her eyes open. I wiggle my toes again.

Gray eyes connect with mine. The brows above them arched.

I smile before pouting. *Please?*

Warm hands encase my left foot. Heat pours in.

"How are your feet this cold?" Kaleb tuts, shaking his head, but his hands don't stop massaging.

A shrug is the only answer he gets.

"Either of you ladies ready for bed yet?"

"No," we chorus.

Kaleb's chuckle is breathy and tired. He's ready for bed.

I nudge his thigh with my other foot. "You should go on up."

He looks at me as if I have six heads.

"I didn't sleep this morning when you were too excited to sleep. What makes you think I'd leave you two now at"—he pauses to check his watch—"eight thirty at night."

Guilt hits me hard. "But it's a boy," I remind him.

"Woohoo," Shelby whisper-shouts, her hand slips out from her huddle and waves a blue flag on a stick that we made. Mine lay abandoned on the coffee table.

Mom texted during breakfast that Charlie had given birth to a small but healthy baby boy. Name to be announced. *Spoilsports.*

Kaleb had been his usual fun self and helped us make some blue flags for when we FaceTimed with our brother. He rarely tells me no.

Daniel had been the picture of relief and stress . . . and then shock when we called with party horns and flags.

At that point, Shelby and I had gone past tired-ness and straight into delirious energy. No one slept.

We talked Kaleb into a movie day and haven't moved since.

"I think he did sleep." I nod, looking at Shelby for support.

"Unless he snores while awake."

I nod. "Definitely heard snoring."

"You did not," he protests.

"Did, too." I insist, poking him with my foot again.

"Did not!"

His fingers skim along the sole of my foot, and a giggle escapes before I glare.

"Don't you dare," I warn.

He leans sideways so that his torso is over my body and whispers, "Oh, I dare."

His fingers attack, ripping a squeal from me, then he straightens like it never happened.

"Did I snore?" he asks.

I pull my feet back from his lap, curl my legs in, and turn to my right side, facing the television.

"Yes." I nod. "Like a rhino."

Loud fake snoring noises fill the room, but a solid swat to my ass makes me laugh. Something that I wouldn't do if the blanket wasn't there to soften the blow.

Kaleb likes nothing more than discipline, especially in his own house.

"Thank you for letting us stay," I whisper gratefully.

Keeping my eyes on the film, I stretch out again, just enough to tuck my still cold feet beneath his right thigh.

"Bed at ten," Kaleb announces, his right hand settling on the outside of my left thigh.

We settle again, the sound of the movie and rain hitting the windows the only thing breaking the silence.

"I can't believe I'm not watching a horror on Halloween." He shakes his head in disappointment.

CHAPTER SEVEN

Samantha

A loud clang jolts me from sleep. My heart pounds as panic floods me.

What was that?

I hold my breath. A streak of light fills my room, and the loud noise sounds again.

Thunder and lightning.

My heart hammers more.

I reach for the edge of my covers to go in with my mom and dad. As I do, the room lights up again.

White duvet. This isn't my room. I'm at Kaleb's.

My eyes water, and I lie back down.

Come on, Sam. You got this. Twenty-two and afraid of storms. Pathetic.

My eyes search the dark room, fear consuming me. *I can do this.*

Thunder rumbles again. *I can't do this.* Ripping the covers back, I rush across the room and out into the hall. I don't stop until I'm outside Kaleb's bedroom, my fist raised.

Something stops me.

The corner of my lip disappears between my teeth. *Maybe Shelby will cuddle with me?* My arm drops. Will he even let me? Things between us have been . . . weird lately. After the whole driving his car into a tree thing last year, Kaleb got . . . stricter. Black and white, no room for gray.

My right hand drifts back to touch my ass.

He stopped being as playful, and I lost my partner in crime, at least for a while. For the past few months, he's been my Kaleb again. Strict but fair. I rarely got in trouble because he was usually helping me. A year ago, I wouldn't debate this. I'd have already been in his room.

Something sad settles in my stomach, so my feet turn to go to the other bedroom, but I don't go more than a few steps. I don't want to cuddle with Shelby. I want Kaleb.

Noise outside makes my feet move before my brain can argue again.

"Kaleb," I whisper into the dark room.

Silence follows.

"Kaleb," I call a little louder, poking my head inside.

My knuckle knocks against the slightly ajar wooden door.

He shoots up in bed, the covers pooling at his hips. My eyes roam his bare chest without permission.

Swallowing hard, I tear my eyes away and meet his dazed stare.

"What are you doing?"

"It's thundering," I offer as if it explains everything.

I guess it does because Kaleb's shoulders sag.

"Go back to sleep, Sam," he tells me, his words muffled as he scrubs his face.

"I want to sleep in here," I whine.

"No." He shakes his head.

"Kaleb, I'm scared," I plead. I'm not above begging.

"This house is safe. You cannot sleep in here, Samantha."

My throat catches, and I search for something that will convince him. Anything. "I'll get the next spider you have?" I offer.

"I'm not afraid of spiders. That's Michael." He sighs, lying back down.

"Oh." My shoulders sag. That's all I have.

I stand in the open doorway, watching as he settles with his right arm bent behind his head.

He's really going to send me away.

"Kaleb." It comes out croaked.

A heavy sigh expands his chest, drawing my attention again. Who knew a man who eats as much as Kaleb could have that many abs?

"I swear to fucking God, woman. You'll be the death of me."

Rude.

"Get in here."

Better.

I don't try to hide my smile. I click the door closed as quietly as I can and run toward his bed. The covers are pulled back on the right side for me when I jump in beside him.

"Thank you." I kiss his cheek.

He doesn't answer, just grunts and rolls away onto his left side. Giving a mental shrug, I pull the blankets high beneath my chin. His scent surrounds me. Pulling a little more on the blankets, I bring them to my nose.

This is creepy, right? But I inhale again, my limbs melting one by one with each inhale.

My breath catches when lightning flashes through the small window. My legs shift restlessly.

I hate storms.

"Samantha," he warns, sounding pretty annoyed. I forgot how grumpy he is when he's tired.

Lying on my back, I worm my body closer to Kaleb's. His warmth pours out, inviting and forbidden.

Don't make it weird, Sam.

I don't stop moving until I feel his back against my arm. When thunder rumbles again, the bed shakes with how hard I jump.

Kaleb's sigh fills me with guilt.

A thick arm reaches back, his large hand clasps my right hip rolling me until my front is pressed against his back. The bed shakes again.

"Easy, sweet girl. The only thing dangerous in this room is me. Nothing and no one gets past me to get to you," he whispers, stroking his thumb back and forth along the band of my shorts.

But it's not fear that shakes my body this time, and my eyes tear up as I swallow my secret. My breathing stutters, fanning his back. A streak of lightning shows the goose pimples I've caused.

The hand on my hip shifts, dropping to my lower back. His fist is harsh when he grabs a handful of my shorts and tank top. The cotton rides up as he pulls.

My body rises, gliding over his clumsily.

"Ahh." I squeak in pain. My shorts and panties are bunched in my ass crack. I have the world's biggest wedgie. "You could have just asked," I grumble.

"And you could be in your own bed." He huffs, shifting me until I land on the bed in front of him. "Turn," he orders, pointing away from himself.

I do as I'm told. We're both too tired for me to argue.

Reaching back, I try to fish my clothes from my ass. The back of my hand grazes something a second before his hand grips mine tightly. His tone is sharp as he says, "Stop."

"I'm uncomfortable." I roll my eyes.

I feel him shrug behind me. "And I was sleeping before you came in."

"Well, I wasn't wearing a thong," I snap, finally adjusting my shorts when he releases his hold.

His chuckle is deep and sleepy. It forces any remains of fear from my body. It takes a few minutes, but he slowly relaxes too.

A strong arm snakes over my ribs, pulling me close. His chest to my back makes my nipples pebble, and I fight what he makes me feel, but I don't fight for long. Sleep consumes me quickly once I'm wrapped up safely in his arms.

But even as I rest, the storm outside isn't the only one that rages. A tear leaks out, rolling over the bridge of my nose and dropping onto the pillow.

The pillow that smells like him . . . the man who I can never have.

CHAPTER EIGHT

Samantha

For the second time tonight, I jolt awake. My harsh breathing fills the room while my heart tries to beat its way out of my chest.

"Shhh," a deep voice rumbles as a large hand soothes back and forth on my stomach, kicking my blood pressure up another notch.

Kaleb.

Wetting my lips, I turn my head to look at the man pressed against my side, his head resting on my pillow. I'm lying on my back, so he no longer spoons me. Instead, he's cuddled close to my side.

Eyes closed, Kaleb nudges his nose with mine. "I'm right here. Go back to sleep," he whispers.

My mind responds to the order, but my body fights him. Heat spreads through me, starting all down my right side where he touches me. My cheeks flush, and my body tingles. I have never been more aware of him.

His hot breath fans my face, and my eyes drop closed. What would happen if I closed the gap?

As if he heard me, his eyes pop open.

Drawing in a breath, I start to speak, but the palm on my stomach shoots up and clamps down on my mouth.

Kaleb's large body rolls, his weight pinning me to the mattress. His left index finger settles over his lips.

Startled, I don't even breathe. All sound in the room stops. That's when I hear it. Metal jingles downstairs.

What the fuck is that?

Steely gray eyes stare down into my terrified blue.

Someone's breaking in! I swallow the lump in my throat.

Kaleb's eyes dip to my throat, and a look I can't place settles on his face, but a second later, it's gone, and so is he.

Climbing out of bed, Kaleb speaks quietly. "You will go into my bathroom and lock the door. I'll lock the bedroom door. You come out for no one but me."

I watch in silence as he calmly opens his bedside drawer and pulls out a large kitchen knife.

He keeps that in his fucking drawer? *Why?* My question is answered when a noise downstairs draws my attention.

Fingers on my chin turn my face back to his.

"You will go into that bathroom and lock the door. Now is not the time to disobey me, Samantha. The punishment I give you will be unlike any other."

I nod, words refusing to come.

Kaleb nods back. Leaning in, he places a soft kiss on my forehead.

"I'll call the police?" I force out.

At the bedroom door, Kaleb pauses, turning back. "No."

I shiver at the smirk he gives me, and my nipples bead.

And then he's gone. The wood silently closes, and metal clicks as the door locks.

My harsh breaths echo in the room, my eyes searching for something to grab. What if the person comes upstairs?

Then Kaleb's dead.

My eyes fill, and tears flow out. I look around for his cell so I can call the police, but Kaleb's refusal repeats in my head.

Oh God, what do I do?

CHAPTER NINE

Kaleb

I place the key back on top of the doorframe, hidden from sight. Easy to find? Maybe, but they'd have to get past me first, and that's not happening.

I hear her before I see her. Turning to the left, I see Shelby peek out of the spare room nervously.

"Kaleb," she whispers, "I think . . ." Her eyes shift to the wall hiding the stairs.

I nod, confirming her suspicions, and walk over to her with a finger raised to my lips. When I'm close enough, I lower my head and whisper into her ear, "Go into the bathroom and lock the door. I'll lock this one. You only unlock the door for me."

Panic and fear consume her face.

"Hey," I call. "Over my dead body."

I watch to make sure she does as told, happy when she doesn't fight me.

"Kaleb." She pokes her head out of the bathroom. "You're the brother I never had. You know that, right?" Surprise fills me. Shelby and I hang out all the time because the girl is always with Sam. I hadn't realized she felt this way, but I'm glad she does. "I can't lose another family member, so don't die, or I'll kick Sam's ass."

"You're not losing anything," I vow before securing her door.

I've always wanted a sister to have the type of relationship that my brothers have with Samantha.

Samantha is your sister.

The fuck she is! I argue with myself.

As the only biological child of Helen and Christopher Cromwell, Samantha and I share no blood. Our bond is different from that of my brothers and me. We never clicked, never formed that kind of love. As we got older, we found a rhythm that worked for us . . . until it didn't.

Now, I spend my days wanting to be around her but working so much that I can't. Some things just shouldn't be, but that woman owns me, and if I can't have her mind, body, and soul, I'll settle for what I can get.

Sam loves me. I know that, and even if it's not the type of love I crave, it's enough. It'll have to be.

Frustration and disappointment fill me but so does

excitement. I'm about to have an outlet for that frustration.

The stairs lead down into the living room. If the intruder came through the front, there's no way for me to surprise them. They'll have the upper hand.

Creeping down the stairs, I strain my ears. Where are they? How many are there? My back stays plastered to the wall. The hilt of the knife feels familiar in my right hand.

Noise drifts out from the kitchen. *They came in through the back.* Stepping off the stairs, I slip through the dining room door and into the laundry room. The door leading to the kitchen is open just a crack.

One guy. Someone breaks in to my house, and they choose to do it alone? *No, not alone.*

I hear someone move farther into the house. The living room. There are two uninvited guests. One of which is closer to my girls than I'd like.

I move quickly and quietly, going back the way I just came. My bare feet are silent on the wood flooring as I approach from behind. He doesn't hear a thing, too busy opening drawers and looking through the papers inside. He's big, but I'm bigger.

My left arm wraps around his head and pulls it to the left, exposing his neck. The balaclava he's wearing makes it easier to grip him. I raise my right hand up, then slam it down. I repeat the motion over and over as fast as I can. Short, sharp stabs slick his neck.

Blood spurts out the side of his neck like a broken water pipe. A gurgle is the only sound in my living room other than my panted breaths. My whole body shivers when I plunge the knife in again.

I've missed this.

There's no other feeling like it.

Freedom, excitement, and arousal.

His body slumps, and I'm forced to catch his weight. I can't have his friend hearing.

Shit, he's heavy.

The flashlight in his right hand drops. My eyes widen as I watch it fall in slow motion. My breath catches. *Shit.* Relief fills me at the same time as air inflates my lungs when the torch lands silently on the living room rug.

I smile as I tug his dead weight out of the room and into the dining room. My mind wanders to one of the women upstairs and all the trouble I gave her over the decor. I hate that fucking rug.

I owe Sam an apology and a shopping trip with my card. She can buy whatever the fuck she wants.

My girl did good.

My girl.

My eyes slip closed for just a second. I shouldn't have thought of her, not while I'm . . . busy. The cotton pajama pants I have on start to shift. My hard cock stands out in the loose-fitting pants.

Not the time.

Dropping the body carefully, I rip the mask off. *I don't know him.* I wasn't expecting to, but I need to make sure that this break-in is random. The only way to do that is to get answers.

Thankfully, I only need one to be breathing for that.

Reaching down, I allow myself a second to grab and squeeze my hard-on. Later. First, I need answers.

The other robber is calling out for his friend. His voice rings out through the lower level.

"Mark! Mark!"

I frown at his volume. He's not being quiet. Realization dawns. I came back early. They didn't know I was home. So they're not here for me. Then what the fuck do they want?

I'd been joking earlier, but really, what are the odds they come here?

My eyes drift to the ceiling and the ladies above. This needs to be quick and quiet.

The knife is slippery and wet, but I've never been more in my element. I twist the handle over and over as I approach the kitchen through the laundry room. The second man is distracted because he's looking for his friend, so I can approach him from behind.

Maybe it doesn't need to be too quick.

The blade catches the moonlight before it cuts through the jacket covering his arm. I know I got skin when he hisses. He whips around frantically.

Hidden in the shadows, I stay out of view, bathing in the fear that pours off him. He should be afraid. I'm nowhere near done.

Stepping out of the darkness, I swing for him again. This time, I catch him across the face. His balaclava does nothing to stop the blade.

The beam of his flashlight blinds me for a second, and it's all he needs. He's quicker than I expected.

"Ugh."

The little fucker's shoulder connects with my stomach, knocking the wind out of me, and the force sends us both into the kitchen cabinet. The doors clang, and a jar on the counter shatters when my arm shoots back to steady myself.

Glass explodes across the tiled floor.

I stab wildly at his back with shallow strikes that force him to retreat. The glass crunches under his boots, but the shards cut and embed in my bare feet when I follow. Our blood mixes on the white floor.

Fucker!

Slouched forward, he's injured but not dying, not yet at least. I don't know if he senses what's coming or doesn't like his odds, but his eyes flit to the back door. Not a chance. To get there, he has to pass me.

I sneer. *I dare you.*

He darts to the right through the doorway leading to the living room. He's not making it to the front door.

My body slams into his, driving him into the wood with as much force as I can. He grunts before slumping to his knees.

Grabbing his shoulder, I force him over so he's sitting on his ass. Gasping for breath, he leans on the door.

I rip off the mask and spit, "Who sent you?"

He shakes his head, coughing. Blood splatters his chin.

"You didn't come here on a whim. Why are you in my fucking house?"

No answer. I stab the knife into the muscle of his thigh, earning a scream. Ripping it out, I lift the knife again, aiming for the other leg.

"Wait, wait, wait," he begs, his hands stretched toward me.

"Who?"

"I don't know."

I raise my brow and shrug, the knife lowering to my next target.

"No, no! Mark chooses where we hit. He talked to some guy. He paid us four hundred to search this place. Find any safes or Halloween costumes. The guy was a fucking weirdo, but I don't know his name."

I believe him. *Fuck!* I should have killed this one first. *Rookie mistake, Kaleb.*

Grabbing the collar of his jacket, I rip him away from the door. His body drops like it's lined with cement.

Standing tall, I roll my head on my shoulders, walking behind as he crawls forward, leaving a trail of blood on my hardwood floor. Stepping over his body, I cut off the world's slowest exit.

"Please," he begs, changing direction. "He was a cop."

I freeze, stunned. *It can't be.*

"A cop?" I repeat.

He nods frantically. "I don't know his name, but he said he used to be a cop. He's not anymore. Is that enough?" he cries.

"Yeah." I nod. "That's enough. We're done." *I know who it was. Fucking Cooper.*

Michael should have let Daniel and me kill him years ago.

I stand at the bottom of the stairs as he drags himself up, step by step. He's determined, I'll give him that. But a promise is a promise. We're done. I don't need him anymore.

My feet scream in pain as the glass that's lodged in presses deeper. The carpet on the stairs is rough against my open wounds.

My bare chest heaves as I stab my way up his legs and back. The hum in my body grows with every injury that I inflict.

By the time I'm done, he lies motionless, and I'm euphoric.

CHAPTER TEN

Kaleb

I leave the home invaders where they lay, blood seeping into my carpet and floors. That's going to be a bitch to get out. I need to call the sheriff and report the break-in, but first, I have a couple of other things to take care of.

A slap sounds when I slam my blood-covered hand on the wall, dragging it downward leaving a desperate handprint behind.

At the top of the stairs, I kick over the side table holding a vase of flowers. It tumbles to the floor with a loud bang. Ceramic and water spill out.

I was defending the girls, Sheriff. I had no choice.

Chuckling, I add another handprint, this time reaching around to grab the edge of the wall at the top of the stairs, making it look as if I was rushing to get up here first.

That'll do.

The first-floor landing is dark and quiet. I should probably get the girls together and ready for the police, but there's one more thing to do.

At my bedroom door, I glance down. The front of my pants is tented, my cock harder than it's ever been. I'm not waiting for the town's subpar police department to do interviews before I take myself in hand.

My balls are fucking killing me.

Reaching up for the key, I hiss as the muscles on my back stretch. Who knew being body-slammed into the kitchen cabinet would hurt like a motherfucker.

I love it. Excitement and adrenaline continue to pump through my body. I push the door open, and anger joins them.

"Why the fuck are you not in the bathroom?" I hiss.

Samantha sits exactly where I left her, perched in the middle of my bed. A vision I would normally kill for. The thought only adds fuel to my fire. A vision I can't fucking have.

Why not?

"Get out."

My words seem to pull her out of her own thoughts.

"Oh my God. Whose blood is that?" She scurries to kneel, crawling across the bed to get closer to me, but I walk around the bottom of the frame, out of reach.

"Mostly theirs," I say dryly, nodding toward the door. Sam drops down to sit, and my eyes follow, taking in all of her exposed skin. Tilting my head back, I pray for more self-control.

"For once in your fucking life, will you please do as you're told? Go to your room." Tearing my gaze away, I go to the en suite.

"Kaleb," she calls tearily.

She's worried, and I know that, but what very little control I usually have on myself is gone. I need her out of reach.

The sound of my name leaving her mouth, the fear and her pain cut through my resistance even more. I'm hanging by a fucking thread. I reach up and grip the doorframe. The pain in my back arouses me more.

She needs to leave before I snap.

"I'm going to take a piss. If you're still here when I come out, I'm going to fuck you like a whore. Brutal and unforgiving. Your Kaleb isn't coming out of this bathroom, Samantha." Glancing over my shoulder, I meet her shocked blue gaze. "Don't be here."

CHAPTER ELEVEN

Samantha

I sit there stunned. Fuck me? Has he lost his goddamn mind?

My chest heaves, the air suddenly thick, and my panties moisten.

We have never spoken about this thing between us. It's dark and shameful. I wasn't even sure if he felt it.

I guess now I know.

A splash of red on the door burns into my vision. Blood. *Theirs.* That's what he had said. Are they dead? My head turns from the bedroom door back to where Kaleb disappeared.

I hear the toilet flush, and my body reacts without permission. One second, I'm sitting bewildered on the bed, and the next, I'm on my feet, frantically looking around.

What the fuck do I do? I can't be here when he comes out, right? *Of course I fucking can't. Can I?*

While my mind is busy arguing with itself, the decision is made for me when the bathroom door opens.

My brain turns off, and all rational thought leaves me.

I should leave. I know I should. Instead? I drop and roll.

I barely fit under the wooden bed. Silently, I lay on my stomach, covering my mouth with my hand when Kaleb's bare feet appear to the right of me.

Air lodges in my lungs, refusing to leave. My whole body is afraid that he'll catch me.

Is it fear? I don't answer the little voice in the back of my mind. I don't have to. We both know I'm sopping wet.

My brows furrow. There's fresh blood on the soles of his feet.

Mostly theirs. Mostly.

Kaleb's injured, and my guts twist. I should help him. This is silly. The man just protected Shelby and me. Why am I hiding under his bed like he's some kind of animal?

I roll my eyes. I'm so dramatic. Stretching my arm out toward him, I open my mouth but snap it shut as his pajama pants pool at his ankles.

I snatch my arm back.

Heat flushes my face, spreading down my neck to my chest the second his loud groan fills the room.

"Fuck," he pants.

Oh. My. God.

My face and chest aren't the only things heating up. My lower stomach flares, my clit pulses, and my pussy weeps.

Kaleb pants, his feet disappearing from my vision when he moves toward the end of the bed. Squeezing my eyes closed, I cover my ears, but there's no blocking out his pleasure-filled pants.

I hear him spit and hiss again, his tugging frantic.

"Sam."

It's quiet and moaned, but the sound of my name is clear. My ears ring.

I gasp in shock.

The room stills. *Oops.*

"Ahhh," I scream, startled when a hand clamps around my right ankle.

"What did I say, Samantha?" Kaleb chuckles. I barely recognize his voice. Husky and deep, it pulls at my core.

Another scream rips from me when he starts to pull me out from under the bed. I claw at the wooden floor, desperate to gain leverage.

It's useless. My nails scratch, my top bunching under my breasts. Large hands clamp onto my thigh for better leverage and pull me the rest of the way out.

Kaleb lifts my hips, forcing me to my knees.

Strong fingers rip at my shorts, shoving them over my ass and down my legs as far as they'll go with how I'm positioned.

"Kaleb, wait!" I plead. "It's me, Sam."

I reach back blindly to pull up my shorts and panties, but his hand just knocks mine away with a sharp slap. The sound of his hand hitting my ass registers before I feel it.

"It's Sam." I try again, my voice turning teary.

Kaleb's large body folds over mine, his hot breath hits my face a second before his hips hit mine. "I know exactly who you are," he growls.

His body plunges into mine with one solid stroke. His thick cock knocks what little air I have in my body out.

My mouth opens with a silent scream.

Holy fuck.

I suck in air when he retreats, but his hips slam against my ass, quickly forcing it from my body. Over and over. Kaleb thrusts his large cock into me. Frantic, almost mean.

Our moans mix with the sound of our hips meeting.

The rug is rough against my cheek, and the friction is harsh. Turning my head, I push up onto my hands, shoving my hips back to meet Kaleb thrust for thrust.

"Kaleb, stop," I order, but even as the words leave my mouth, I rock back, needing more of him.

"Stop, huh?" He chuckles. The large hands gripping my hips move. His left hand slides up my ribs, beneath my yellow top, and around to grab my breast, squeezing tightly and then releasing. Every time his palm rubs my nipple, it sends a shock of pleasure to my clit. His right hand holds my right shoulder. Using the leverage it gives him, Kaleb yanks me back onto him with so much force that it's painful.

"It doesn't feel like you want me to stop," he pants. His body folds over mine, and his hands bracket me in. "No," he breathes in my ear, "it feels like you want me to keep fucking this wet pussy."

His hips never stop. My inner walls contract at his words.

Desperate sounds leave me. This is so wrong, but fuck, I need him.

"No, no, no." I shake my head, but my body's actions contradict my words as we work together, desperate to find the finish line.

Kaleb pulls his chest away from my back, tangling his hand in my hair. My neck strains when he pulls the fistful of blond locks.

"Yes, yes, yes," he chants, fucking me. "This is happening, you and me. That dick inside you is mine, those moans you're making are mine. The cum I'll fill you with is mine. You're mine, Samantha. Always have been, always will be."

His words, the smell, the sound, it's all too much. The hand on my hip slides under me. His middle finger barely touches my clit, but it's enough. One minute, I'm hanging on the edge of something power-ful, and the next, I'm flying.

This time, my scream isn't silent. It pierces the air at the same time Kaleb's cum fills me. His roar continues as he pumps everything he has into me. My body tenses, and my womanhood quivers.

Tears leak out as his essence spills down my inner thigh.

My upper body collapses in relief and grief, and with my forehead resting on my arms, my body is rocked back and forth.

Biting my wrist, I try to smother my sobs.

One final grunt sounds behind me, and Kaleb stills. His hands settle on my hips, the soft caress of his thumbs on my ass a completely one-eighty to the way he touched me just seconds before.

I fucked Kaleb. I fucked my brother.

The thought sets off another round of sobs.

Cries and panting fill the room.

I can't catch my breath.

"I'm done fighting this, Sam."

His cock starts to leave me, but he slowly pushes it back in.

"That's my cum," he tells me as semen drips out around his manhood. "That's my pussy, and you're my woman."

His words make my body heat, and the pulse in my clit starts anew. A war rages inside me, my mind and body on opposite sides.

Our groans echo as he pulls from my used body. I

cringe as my inner walls continue to pulse. I feel empty and lost without him.

A smack sounds out, and my ass cheek stings. "Put some sweatpants on. We're going to the cabin once the cops get here."

My cries have simmered to sniffles. I wipe my face with the back of my hand, refusing to look up as Kaleb stands.

I hear him move to his dresser and retrieve some clothes. I'm still on the floor with my ass in the air when he walks out the door.

What the fuck have we done?

CHAPTER TWELVE

Kaleb

I walk out without looking back at Samantha. If I don't, I'm not sure I can walk away without fucking her again.

The sight of her filled to the brim is forever burned into my brain.

My shirt feels foreign beneath my palm as I rub my chest. I feel different, calmer. Something deep inside me settled the minute I entered her body.

I feel weird. Happy.

Giving a breathy laugh, I reach up for the key and open Shelby's door.

My smile fades as I remember the way Sam had cried. *It's just new. She'll get used to it. Used to us.*

The spare bedroom is dark and empty.

At least one of the girls can take direction. I roll my eyes.

"Shelby, it's Kaleb," I call through the bathroom door.

Raising my hand, I go to knock, but the door flings open, and the petite brunette barrels into my chest. I groan in pain as she clings to me.

Hearing me, she loosens her hold and pulls back enough to look up at me with watery blue eyes.

"Everything's okay. You're safe." I smile, stroking the back of her hair. Pulling her into my chest, I hug her close. Poor girl looks terrified. Remembering her earlier words, I drop a kiss on the top of her head. "You're okay," I repeat firmly.

Shelby sniffles. "Are you?" Her hands run over my back as if she's looking for something. "Are you injured?"

"Nothing a shower and antiseptic won't cure."

"What's going on here?"

At Sam's sharp words, I spin with Shelby still in my arms. My girl is standing in the doorway, and she looks mad.

Something else settles in my stomach besides my earlier contentment. Samantha's jealous . . . and I fucking love it.

"Hi, baby." She flinches at the endearment. "We're just cuddling. Come join," I explain, holding my arm out wide.

Sam shakes her head, looking back and forth between her friend and me.

"Come on, Sammy." Shelby motions with her right hand for Samantha to join us.

Hesitant, slow steps bring her to us, and the three of us stand hugging in the middle of the room.

"We should call the police," Sam mumbles, her eyes not meeting mine.

"Already did." Shelby smiles, lifting her left arm and shaking something.

My hand clamps down sharply on her wrist.

"When the fuck did you do that?"

Shelby shrugs, frowning when I glare at her lack of answer.

"Umm, I don't know. I mean, I was scared. I waited in the bathroom, but I wanted to know what was happening, so I snuck in here to get my phone. I went straight back to the bathroom," she rushes to tell me, her thumb pointing back to where she had been.

"And then you called the police," I finish for her.

"No." She shakes her head. "I text Sam to check that she was okay, but she didn't answer. I would have called, but I didn't want to give away her hiding spot," she rambles.

"And then you called?" I ask.

"And then I called." She nods. "I'm sorry," Shelby whispers, confused at my annoyance.

"It's okay." I sigh, pulling her back into my chest.

And it is. She was just trying to help. But now I don't know how long I have to stage a scene, which means I have no time. Someone suspecting I moved things around is one thing, but getting caught is another.

The work I did earlier will have to do.

I use the excuse of comforting Shelby to hug Sam close too. The three of us stand there for a few more seconds before I hear movement downstairs.

I don't move. Instead, I up the reassurance, making it obvious that I'm here to comfort the girls. After all, I did just save us all from intruders.

"You're both okay."

The local sheriff and several officers from Cromwell's Police Department enter with guns drawn. Seeing us huddled in the middle of the room, they lower their weapons.

"What's going on, son?" Sheriff McCallister asks, his voice shaking. "We got a call about a home invasion, but downstairs is, is . . ." He struggles for words.

"A fucking massacre," one of the officers whispers.

I don't know if it's his words, the realization of what could have happened, or emotions from what we did in my bedroom, but Sam breaks at his words. Gut-wrenching sobs shake her body.

I pull her so that her face is buried in my chest and kiss the top of her head. Shelby rubs her back before stepping away.

"Where are you going?" Before she can answer, I crouch and order them both, "Arms around my neck and hold on tight."

Neither lady does as they were told until I wrap an arm around each of them at the top of their thighs and lift them by their legs.

Shelby gives a short scream and flails for a second,

then latches on to my neck. Sam grips the back of my shirt and hides her wet face in my neck.

"I'm going to need a medic," I tell the sheriff.

Sam makes a distressed sound that's muffled by my skin.

"My feet need the glass removed," I explain to the cops, but my words are for my girl.

"I need to take you in," McCallister starts.

"For what?" I raise a brow. "For defending myself and two young women?"

The older man takes his hat off and runs a hand through the graying hair. "They were unarmed, Kaleb. We already looked."

"They were the weapons," I snap. "They didn't break in here to make themselves dinner. They both attacked, and one tried to get upstairs to these." I motion to the women in my arms.

Shelby's eyes widen, and her mouth falls open. All the color leaves her face.

I almost feel bad.

"You know what? You should arrest me." I nod. "I'd love to see how that plays out in this town. I took care of the two little pricks terrorizing the town, only to get charged for it." I chuckle and move to go past him. "We'll be at my parents' cabin if you need anything else, but I suggest you make it sooner rather than later as these two will be going back to bed shortly."

He's full of shit, and he knows it.

Two of the officers at the door scramble out of

my way, but the third blocks the doorway, "A man has the right to protect his family." Stepping aside, he meets my gaze. "They got what they deserved."

"Officer Kelly, that is enough," McCallister reprimands.

And it is enough. It proves my point. This town would rally behind me.

I leave them to it and move down the hall. I need to get out of here, settle the girls, and call my parents.

I really am going to be the child who gives my dad a heart attack.

Nearing the top of the stairs, I whisper, "Close your eyes, both of you." I watch Shelby close hers and feel Sam's lashes brush my neck. "Good girls. Don't open them until I tell you."

The officer at the bottom of the stairs watches as I carry both women down, stepping over the body like it's just some laundry to be moved later.

"Hand me the car keys please?" I ask another officer, motioning with my chin to where they lay on the coffee table.

The female cop looks behind me, and after a second, she retrieves the keys.

"Hold your right hand out and take the keys. Keep your eyes closed," I say, my right hand squeezing Shelby's thigh.

Blindly, she reaches out, taking the keys. I turn to give the sheriff one last look, then leave.

My bare feet sting. The coldness of the concrete feels good, almost soothing. Neighbors are out in their gardens trying to get a good look at what is happening. It's not every day we have police cars and lights flashing in the middle of the night.

Seeing me, my neighbor Aaron rushes over.

"What happened?"

Ignoring him, I speak to Shelby, "Open your eyes and unlock the car, sweetheart." Then I nod to the car door. "Open that, please," I ask Aaron.

Ducking, I gently place Shelby into the car. "Hand me the keys and scooch over," I urge her, placing Sam on the seat when there's room.

Climbing into the driver's seat, I finally answer my neighbor. "A home invasion. They attacked. I wasn't supposed to be home. The girls were supposed to be here house-sitting, alone," I lie, stressing the last word. "I don't know what they were looking for, but they didn't get it." I glance back at the girls, hoping that he would follow my train of thought.

He does.

His eyes widen, and horror and guilt fill his face. "I didn't hear anything."

I wouldn't expect him to. It's one of the reasons I bought a house on this street. All of the houses are far enough away from each other so that you get privacy. As much as you're going to get in a small town, anyway.

"It's not your fault. Besides, I took care of it. They won't be bothering anyone else."

Aaron nods, looking back at Shelby and Sam. "Good, that's good."

"Listen, I need to get to my parents' cabin and have my injuries looked at. You take care of yourself and lock your house up tight. This town's not as safe as it used to be," I mutter, looking back at my house.

Aaron follows my gaze and harrumphs when he sees the sheriff. "I'll say."

I give a wave and pull off, hissing when I press the gas pedal. My feet really do fucking hurt.

"Which one of you is helping me clean and wrap my feet?" I ask.

When I get no answer, I look back through the rearview mirror.

Sam looks away quickly while Shelby's wide eyes lock with mine.

Denial and shock.

Not having the energy to deal with both right now, I choose shock.

"You heard what I said to Aaron?" I ask Shelby, and the young woman nods. "We stick with that," I tell her sternly.

"Why?" she whispers.

"Because I don't feel like going to prison for killing two people."

Her cheeks flush at my words.

"But you saved us."

"They were unarmed," I say, repeating Sheriff McCallister's words.

"They attacked you?" Shelby argues, but her tone makes it sound like a question.

"They did." I nod. "And they were coming

upstairs. I told you I wouldn't let anything happen, and I didn't."

Shelby's bottom lip disappears between her teeth, her bright eyes shining with unshed tears. The car stays quiet until I pull up in front of the dark cabin.

"We were house-sitting for you." Shelby nods.

Good girl.

"I came home early, and we're lucky I did. Samantha?"

"We were house-sitting," she agrees, never turning away from the side window.

My chest expands with a heavy sigh. "Both of you stay there. I'll carry you out."

"We can walk," Sam argues.

"You're both barefoot."

"So are you."

Fed up, I turn in my seat. "Samantha, I'm tired and exhausted. Just stay in the car." My tone is sharp enough that her eyes snap to mine. She quickly looks away.

Fuck.

I climb out of the car and brush off her attitude. It doesn't matter how bratty she gets. It won't take back what we did. Grinning, I open the back door.

CHAPTER THIRTEEN

Samantha

My stomach roils, and it's not because of the blood seeping into the gauze held to Kaleb's foot.

"I think I'm going to vomit," Shelby grimaces, turning away from where Kaleb sits on the closed toilet.

"You good?" he asks her.

Shelby shakes her head. Her face paling.

"Woman, I'm good with killing to protect you, but if you vomit on me, there will be a third murder tonight."

"Why do you have so much blood? It just keeps coming."

Kaleb laughs, turning to me. "Baby, pass me some more gauze, please."

I blink at him.

"Sam," he urges, nodding at the first-aid kit.

I walk over on numb legs.

"Thank you." He smiles, his fingers brushing mine as I pass the gauze. "I'm nearly done. Shelb got all the glass out. I'm just going to clean the cuts and bandage my feet."

"I'm going to lie down," Shelby says, staggering to her feet.

Catching her elbow, I walk her to the door.

"Hey, sis," Kaleb calls.

I freeze at his words, my world crumbling. Eyes filled with tears, I turn, but it's not me Kaleb looks at. Instead, he smiles softly at Shelby.

"Thanks for helping me out."

Shelby gives a small thumbs-up and continues into the hall.

Standing in the doorway, I look back at Kaleb.

"Go, make sure she's okay."

I nod, not needing to be told twice.

"Samantha," he calls just before I round the corner, "this isn't going away."

My chin wobbles. Swallowing hard, I straighten my back.

He's wrong. It is going away. As of right now, nothing happened in that bedroom. Nothing.

CHAPTER FOURTEEN

Kaleb

My head shoots up when I hear the front door open.

Ripping the tape off with my teeth, I seal the bandage that covers the sole of my foot and hobble out of the bathroom just in time to see our parents storm in.

"Kids! Kids!" My mom's frantic cries pull at my heart. Her worry doesn't leave even when she spots Sam and Shelby on the sofa. "Girls!"

Rushing forward, Mom wraps Sam in a bear hug.

How did they know? I open my mouth to ask the question aloud, but I'm cut off when Dad sidesteps the hugging women and chokes me with his own hug. I groan. My body aches now that my adrenaline has left.

"You're hurt." Dad's face is horrified.

Holding my shoulders, he pulls back to look me over.

"Mom," Sam groans, trying to escape the barrage of kisses being planted all over her face. Shelby chuckles but quickly pales and sits back down.

She really does have a weak stomach.

"How did you find out?" I ask Dad.

He tilts his head, his eyes tracing me as if he can see the damage under my T-shirt. "McCallister called and told us everything. We got back as quickly as we could."

"Stop hogging all the hugs. It's my turn." a voice complains behind my dad.

Michael playfully shoulders our dad out of the way, but the concern on his face is obvious.

"Come here, baby brother. You did good."

I smile into his shoulder, and my own eyes tear for a second. This means more than he can ever know. Michael hates to be touched. An issue that's gotten better since he met his wife last year, but even with Lara's help, his past still dominates him.

This is the first hug I've shared with my brother.

"You did good," he repeats, slapping my back. When he pulls away, we share a look.

"You did good, Lube," Lara, my sister-in-law agrees, replacing her husband and giving me her own hug.

"Got to stop calling me that." I shake my head.

"Never," she whispers.

I hug her tighter.

"I can't believe those animals tried to hurt my babies," Mom frets, still framing Sam's face.

"I'm okay, too," I declare loudly, holding up my hand. "What are you two doing here? What about Charlie?" I ask my brother and his wife.

"She and baby . . ."

Mom clears her throat, cutting him off. She knows the name. I squint at her.

"Charlie and the baby," Michael says carefully, "are doing great. Momma is catching up on sleep, and Daniel has Belle in the hospital room with them. Lara and I will head back tomorrow to stay until they're ready to come home, probably next week."

"Daniel didn't mind you coming back?"

Michael's head rears back as if I slapped him. "Kaleb, your house was broken into while you were in it. Daniel helped me pack everyone's bags."

I frown, my pride taking a punch. "I had everything covered. No one was getting near Sam or Shelby."

"I wasn't worried about Sam or Shelby. I knew you had them covered. I was worried about you."

Oh.

My cheeks flush, and my heart swells. With how close Michael and Daniel are, sometimes it's easy to forget how much they love me too.

"And it looks like I was right to be." He motions to my feet. "Any other injuries?"

Uncomfortable with the attention of the room, I

shrug nonchalantly. "My ribs and back took a knock, but nothing a hot bath and rest won't fix."

I roll my head on my shoulders. *Sleep and another good fuck too*, I silently add.

My eyes find Sam, but she's still happily bathing in our mother's attention.

"How are you doing, Shelby?" Dad asks, making his way over to her.

Shelby gives a small smile and a hum to show she's okay. The color is finally returning to her cheeks.

"Tonight could have ended so differently," Dad whispers. "We could have lost three of our kids."

Shelby blushes at his words. She's family, and it's good for her to hear it. Her earlier words repeat in my head.

The front door opens again. Michael and I step forward, putting ourselves in front of the family. Sheriff McCallister walks in, following a frantic-looking Dr. Leonard Moore.

"Is everyone okay?" Doc rushes.

"Come on in," Dad says dryly.

Leo slows his steps. Reaching up, he straightens his black-rimmed glasses. "My apologies. I heard what happened, and Jeff said a doctor was needed." He thumbs back to the sheriff, his eyes finding Shelby on the sofa.

"Still, probably shouldn't enter a home without knocking tonight." Michael glares.

"So I hear."

"I need to take everyone's statement," McCallister adds.

"That can't wait?" Dad asks.

"Umm," McCallister mumbles, desperate not to piss off the man who funds his re-election campaigns.

The town's doctor slices the tense atmosphere by walking across the room straight to where Sam and Shelby sit.

"You girls okay?"

Sam nods.

"Sweetheart?" he asks Shelby, kneeling at her feet.

My brows shoot high on my forehead. *Sweetheart?*

Her cheeks flame even more. Definitely getting her color back.

"You're very flushed," he tuts, the back of his fingers brushing her cheek. "Did anyone hurt you? Touch you?"

Shelby shakes her head, looking at the older man through her lashes.

When the fuck did this happen?

I watch the two interact while my parents move over to deal with the sheriff. Michael and Lara head to the porch, Michael's phone already to his ear. He's probably calling Daniel.

"Open," Leo orders, pulling my attention away from my family.

Shelby closes her mouth around a thermometer without complaint. He must feel me staring because he glances at me before turning to Sam.

"How are you? Any injuries you need me to look at." He reaches up to feel her forehead.

"I'm okay. Shook up but okay," Sam answers loud enough for our parents to hear.

"You should have stayed at mine," Leo tells Shelby, checking her temperature.

I raise a brow, silently asking her why she'd be doing that.

Shelby rolls her eyes at me.

"Don't be disrespectful," Doc snaps, the tip of his ears turning red.

Oh shit. It's like that, huh?

"I believe it was meant for me, Doc," I explain, giving her an out.

"Still, it's rude," he mutters, catching her eye.

"Sorry."

"If it wasn't meant for me, it's not me you should be apologizing to," he tells her.

"Sorry, Kaleb."

"No problem, sis." I wink. She's not in trouble with me; her neighbor, however, might be. "You stay over at Doc's house often?"

"No," Shelby rushes.

"But I am her neighbor. She should have come to me if she was afraid."

"Afraid?"

"It's October thirty-first. Shelby always gets antsy around Halloween."

News to me.

"You don't like Halloween?" I ask, confused.

Shelby shrugs flippantly, but I see the way she swallows hard. The doctor is right; she is afraid, and it's not just the burglaries. I think back, but nothing from today stands out. She'd been okay. Tired and restful. Maybe she felt better being in someone else's house. Not that it turned out great.

"You can stay with me for a few more days. It's no problem." I frown.

"It's okay." Shelby smiles. "I'm okay, now. It's just the night of Halloween. The past few have been"—she pauses, looking for the right word—"weird."

I frown. The past few Halloweens have been weird for this family too. Last year, Michael met his wife. The year before that, my brothers' annual hunt didn't happen, and the Halloween before that was the year that Daniel met Charlie.

"Yeah." I chuckle. "Mine too." My eyes trail Sam. "But this year has been by far the most interesting."

"Interesting? Well, that's one word for it," Dad chimes in, the other four returning sans McCallister.

I jut my chin. "He gone?"

"Yeah." Michael nods.

"You kids will have to go down to the station tomorrow to give your statements, but he's going to let you rest for tonight," Dad explains.

"Rest sounds good." Sam yawns.

"Uh-huh." Shelby nods, quickly catching Samantha's yawn.

"I'll drive you home. You can stay at mine. Riley will love waking up to you there," Doc tells her.

Shelby bites her lip.

"I think the girls are best staying together for now. They've been through a lot," I interject.

The doctor doesn't look happy but doesn't argue. I eye the hand he lays on her knee.

"Do you need me to take a look at those feet?" Leonard asks.

"No." I shake my head. "My new bestie got the debris out for me." I grin at Shelby, grateful that she helped despite her hate for blood. "I cleaned the cuts. A few needed paper stitches, but I think they're okay. A couple of painkillers and I'm as good as new."

"Kaleb, don't be stubborn. Let Leonard look while he's here," Mom insists.

Too tired to argue, I drop down onto one of the sofas with a groan.

"What's the longest anyone has ever slept? I think I'm going to break it." I yawn.

I flinch as my feet are unwrapped.

"It's not as bad as I thought it would be." Doc smiles. "You need this one stitched, though. I'll do it now, then come into my office in a few days for a checkup."

Leaning my head back, I nod, closing my eyes.

"Want me to numb it?"

"No," I whisper, losing the fight to stay awake.

A sharp pain jolts me.

Now, I'm awake.

"A home invasion at Kaleb's," Mom mutters, shaking her head.

"Lucky," Michael sulks aloud. Lara hits the side of his thigh. "Lucky that Kaleb was there and able to protect everyone," he fumbles, his eyes flitting the room.

I grin knowingly, throwing my arm along the back of the couch. "Yeah, lucky." I nod at him.

"Boys, this isn't something to be smiling about. Two men died," Dad reprimands.

"Good," Mom blurts. "I'm sorry," she says, holding her hands up and looking anything but sorry. "Those thugs broke into that house wanting to do God knows what, to God knows who. My children are safe, and that's all that matters."

"Hear, hear." Doc nods.

"Daddy, can I sleep in with you and Mom?" Sam asks, her face shrouded in exhaustion. There go my plans for the rest of the night.

"No," Shelby rushes, answering for her. "I want to sleep in your room with you."

"You can stay in with me, Shelbs," I offer.

"No!" Sam snaps. "She's my friend, get your own." For the first time since our family came home, Samantha meets my eyes.

"I do. You," I taunt. I shouldn't, I know that, but she can't avoid me forever. Pain stabs the sole of my foot. "Easy, Doc," I hiss.

"Perhaps, Shelby," he says, stressing her full name, "should leave with me if your sister wants to sleep with your parents."

"Shelby is my sister too. She can sleep wherever the fuck she wants."

Today is not the day to test me. Our gaze holds, a challenge he's not ready for.

"How are his feet, Doc?" Michael asks.

All harshness leaves Leonard's face, his feature softening into a false smile. "All sorted. I'll just bandage them and head out. Keep them dry," he orders.

I give him the same fake politeness back. "Of course. And I'll make an appointment in a few days."

Shelby isn't his, and whether she carries the Cromwell name or not, she's family. He needs to watch himself.

"Okay, babies," Mom calls, grabbing everyone's attention. "Let's start heading to bed, please. Lara, I'll make some muffins for you guys to take back with you tomorrow or later today, I guess." She frowns, looking at the clock.

The heat from the wood fire isn't helping me in my fight to stay awake.

"Thank you. We'll FaceTime you as soon as we get there. It'll be like you're with us."

The room relaxes with my mother's laughter.

Exhausted, I follow the ladies up the stairs while Michael and our dad lock up the house.

Leaning forward, I draw in the smell of vanilla. "Happy Halloween," I whisper next to Sam's ear.

She flinches.

Walking past her, I head to my room without a look back, a smirk firmly planted on my lips.

And what a good Halloween it was.

CHAPTER FIFTEEN

Kaleb

The kitchen is as empty as the rest of the house. Spying a note on the kitchen table, I reach for it.

Taken the girls to the station. Lara and Michael have gone back to the hospital. Eat breakfast. Love, Mom.

Smiling, I place the paper back next to the basket of chocolate chip muffins. Taking a bite, I taper down my disappointment. I was hoping to get Sam alone before we headed out together.

The large clock ticks away on the cream wall.

Five past one, no wonder they went without me. I haven't slept that well in months, but then again, I haven't fucked that hard in a while either. Add in the physical exertion of killing two people, and apparently, you have the recipe for a great night's sleep.

Opening the cupboard on the top right, I grab a

blue mug, and place it under the coffee machine. Flicking it on, I make myself a flat white.

Dropping into a seat, I settle at the table and sip my hot drink. Caffeine is exactly what I need right now. Placing my phone on the table, I stare at it for a minute before snatching it back up. I try not to over-think it as I text Sam.

You okay?

I finish off my muffin and check my phone again. Still no reply. We really do need to work on her carrying that thing with her.

Are you still at the station?

I'm not expecting a reply, but my eye twitches as the hour stretches on. If she doesn't want to talk to me, I'll make her. She's not the only one who needs to go to the police station. Stepping into my sneakers, I text her again.

You can't ignore me forever, baby.

CHAPTER SIXTEEN

Kaleb

My earlier good mood has vanished. They weren't at the station, and McCallister was his usual annoying-as-fuck self. He kept me there for hours, repeating the same questions over and over.

Fuck. Is it too early in the evening to go back to bed and call it a day?

My office clock reads six o'clock. And to top it off, Sam still hasn't texted me back. My eye twitches again.

Toeing out of my shoes, I wiggle my toes. My injured skin stretches. It's not painful, just irritated, like the rest of me.

Opening my top drawer, I search for painkillers, cursing when I find the box empty.

Lifting it high, I wave it, trying to gain Pauline's

attention in the other room. When I do, she gives me a thumbs-up.

Perfect.

Grabbing my cell, I call Samantha. It goes to voicemail again. "Call me back. We need to talk."

Pinching the bridge of my nose, I sigh. Great, I'm getting a tension headache.

I am many things, but patient isn't one of them, so I call again. And again. By the fifth call, I'm beyond irate and throw it on top of my desk.

Fine. She wants to act like a fucking child, then I'll treat her like one. I pick up my cell again, but this time, I scroll to a different name.

"Hey, Kaleb."

"Hi, sweetpea, is she with you?" I ask, trying to match Shelby's light tone.

"Who?"

It seems avoidance is contagious.

I drop all pretense of niceness. "Give Samantha the phone."

"You're on speaker," Shelby murmurs.

"I've been calling and texting you."

The other end of the line stays silent for a second before Sam mumbles, "I don't have my phone."

"We've talked about this, Samantha."

"You're not my fucking dad," she snaps.

My jaw actually drops at her words. "I noticed. The other night made that particularly clear," I shoot back.

Both girls gasp. Did she tell her best friend what happened?

Now is not the time, I remind myself. So I change the subject. "What's this I hear about a belated Halloween party?"

"None of your business," Sam answers.

"Shelby?" I ask, hoping to get more from her.

"I told you that I don't like Halloween. I invited a few friends over, but then the burglaries started happening. Everyone canceled their trick-or-treating plans, so I called off the party."

"So it's canceled? Then why am I hearing about it from Edward's dad?"

The news of a house party at Shelby's nearly sent me over the edge earlier today. Where Shelby is, Samantha isn't far behind.

"Well, it was canceled, but then everyone heard what happened, and they wanted a party to relax. Some of the parents and kids are trick-or-treating today instead, so I thought, why not? It's nothing huge, just a few friends, food, and films. More of a movie night," Shelby rushes to add, but it doesn't make me feel any better.

"No alcohol, and make sure you lock up after everyone leaves. I'm sure you'll have fun, but Samantha won't be there."

The girls respond at the same time.

"Yes, I will!"

"Why not?"

Ignoring Sam's rebuttal, I choose to answer Shelby's question instead.

"She's grounded."

"No, I'm not!"

"Awww, what for?"

Again, I focus on Shelby's question.

"For not having her phone and being unavailable. Clearly having a word about it wasn't enough," I lie. *"I don't want you going to a party without me"* probably wouldn't fly too well.

"You can't ground me. I'm not a fucking child, Kaleb."

"Yet you're acting like one. Stop fucking ignoring me."

"Go fuck yourself," Sam hisses before the line cuts off.

"I'd rather be fucking you," I reply with no one to hear.

Shit.

"Do I even wanna know?" Pauline tuts, pushing my door open, a bottle of water in one hand and a packet of painkillers in the other.

The perfect woman.

"Thank you," I mouth, taking both.

When she sits on the corner of my desk with a raised brow, I shake my head. "Women." That's the only explanation I give.

"Tell me about it," she huffs. "One of the new hires just called out sick again. A woman," she adds when I give a confused look.

"Which one?"

"Justine."

"That's the fourth time this quarter, and we're only a month in," I state.

"I know," she agrees, "hence . . . women." Pauline stands, pushing off my desk. "I need to find someone to take it. Most are already out on jobs."

"I'll take it," I say without thinking.

"What? No, after everything that happened last night, you should be at home resting."

True, but I need space more. "It's fine. My house is trashed, and the cops have not released it yet. I could do with getting out of town for a few days."

"The contract is for Wilder Furniture in Virginia. There and back will be about six days."

Perfect. "How about we call it seven?"

"Want me to book you a motel near Char-lottesville?" Pauline offers.

"No, thank you. I'll sleep in my truck."

Ideas of how to extend my drive pop into my mind, but even now, not knowing where Sam and I stand, the idea of fucking someone else doesn't appeal. I just want her.

Another kill will just have to do.

CHAPTER SEVENTEEN

Kaleb

The sign "Welcome to Cromwell Town" sets off butterflies in my stomach as I pass.

Home sweet home.

Being within the borders of Cromwell has always settled me. Not today.

The past seven days have been hell. I shouldn't have taken the job.

Everything I did made me think of *her*. Settling down for the night; was she sleeping? Stopping at roadside dives; was she eating? Talking to our parents; was she with them? Even fucking driving made me think of her.

My laughter fills the truck cab. She really is a terrible driver—too aggressive, impatient, and arrogant. Something else that's my fault since I did teach her.

Samantha's driving isn't the only thing I'm responsible for. How we left things is too.

I shouldn't have left. I should have confronted this thing head-on. Then again, my girl ignored every single one of my texts and calls while I was gone.

That ends today.

No more ignoring me, ignoring this.

The way things happened was unfortunate, but it did happen. I just need her to stop fighting that fact.

My mind flicks to our family. Michael and Daniel will be okay . . . I think. Michael hinted last year that he would be okay with Sam and me. My throat tightens. I want Sam, but I won't risk losing my family.

Even if our brothers understand and accept my relationship with Sam, our parents will be another story.

Samantha may be Helen and Christopher's only biological child, but I've lived with them since I was eleven. They're the only family I've ever known. Daniel and Michael had been with the Cromwells for a while. They were adopted years before I arrived, but they welcomed me with open arms.

Sam was only six, a brat even then. My lips spread into a grin. We may have shared a childhood home for a portion of our upbringing, but I never bonded with her like I did with the boys. Maybe I wasn't supposed to. Perhaps we were always meant to grow into the relationship we're about to have.

Or maybe my birth mother fucked me up too much.

Who knows? Who the fuck cares?

You do, a small voice whispers. I love Helen and Christopher, so it'll kill me to lose them, but Samantha Cromwell is mine, whether she likes it or not.

I'll make sure she talks to them every day and is at the cabin for lunch every Sunday. Although they're not having her all weekend. Maybe she can travel with me in my truck when I leave for work if I still have a job.

My heart lurches at the possibility of no longer being a Cromwell. One problem at a time.

First, I need to talk to Samantha, and since she's ignoring me, I'm going to get one of the few people she won't ignore.

Shelby.

Pulling into the truck yard, I wave to Marcus as he points me to the spot he wants me to go.

Throwing the truck into park, I reach for my cell.

"Hi, sis. I need a favor . . ."

CHAPTER EIGHTEEN

Kaleb

Turning the front door handle, I silently curse Sam's best friend for not locking the door. Did we not just survive a break-in?

I mean, the woman lives alone now. She should know better.

Shaking my head, I walk through the one-story property until I find Shelby in her bedroom.

Her back to me, she's packing a bag on her bed, completely oblivious that I'm standing in the doorway.

"You and I need to have a word." I tut.

"Ahhh!" she screams. Whipping around, her left hand clutches at her heart while her right lifts the bedside lamp.

"Really?" I ask with a raised brow. "I could be a

serial killer, and your plan is to defend yourself with a lamp?"

"No." She shakes her head, wide-eyed. "The plan is to have a heart attack before I can be murdered. You'll be happy to know we're on schedule."

Shelby tilts her head back and huffs a harsh breath, her cheeks puffing out. She looks like a startled little hamster.

The thought makes me chuckle. *An angry hamster,* I amend.

She glares at me. "How did you even get in?"

I point my thumb behind me. "The door."

Shelby blinks at me. "I'm starting to see why Sam isn't talking to you."

I gasp, clutching my chest. "You get mean when you're scared."

Her body instantly deflates. "I'm sorry. That was mean," she acknowledges. Her fingers move farther up toward her neck, fiddling with something under her shirt. "I locked the front door, is what I should have said."

I frown. "It was unlocked."

Something dark passes over her face, and I don't miss the way her eyes flit about the room.

"I'll check the house."

"Kaleb . . ." she says, her voice sounding unsure.

"It's okay. It'll give me something to do while you finish getting ready."

"Why do I have to be the buffer between you and Sam again?"

"Because you love me like a brother." I smile, stepping out of the bedroom and into the other. "Did she tell you?" I ask from the spare bedroom, not wanting to see the judgment on her face.

But Shelby doesn't answer. I peek into her room as I pass. She's looking at something in her side drawer.

I do a quick sweep of the rest of the house. It's clear, but something still doesn't sit right, and I can't quite put my finger on it. Maybe it's being back in town after what happened last week? I brush off my anxiety and go back to Shelby.

She's still lost in a world of her own, staring into her bedside drawer as I approach.

"I didn't realize that you were seeing someone," I say, looking over her shoulder.

Startled, she slams the drawer shut with her right hand. Her hip whacks the table as she turns to me and stumbles.

I catch her by the arm. "Careful," I chide.

Stretching past her, I tug on the drawer handle, but her hip keeps it closed.

I give her a pointed look.

"What?" she asks innocently.

I don't reply.

"She told me," Shelby says, answering my earlier question about Sam.

She really doesn't want this drawer open.

Straightening, I tower over her.

Shelby cracks first. Side-stepping, she drops her eyes from mine.

Opening the drawer, I look inside. Condoms. The packets are scattered, but it's impossible to miss the clean slit down the middle of each one.

I'd know a knife slice anywhere. Someone piled them high and stabbed right through them. It was small, maybe a scalpel. *Holy shit!*

My gaze snaps back to her, and Shelby flushes. Blush spreads from her cheeks and down her neck. Her hand raises and fiddles with the same object as before.

"Do I need to take care of someone?" I ask carefully.

She quickly shakes her head.

Not good enough.

I catch her chin between my thumb and forefinger. I wait until her eyes meet mine. "Do you need help, Shelby?"

Her teeth chew her lower lip, and her fingers keep fiddling. "No," she finally whispers. "It's complicated."

My hand drops to her collarbone. I hold her gaze captive and slip my finger beneath the chain of the necklace she's been playing with. I pull until the locket rises out of her shirt.

"It was a gift."

I watch her face for a second. She's embarrassed and shy, but she's not lying.

"Okay." I tilt my head to the door. "Let's go make him jealous."

"Why would I want to do that?"

"Because he wants you pregnant before you're ready," I say, motioning to the drawer.

She pouts her lips and squints. "And why would you help me?"

"Because I have someone of my own to make jealous." I grin.

"Are you going to tell Sam about . . ." She motions to the drawer.

I shrug. "I'll keep your secret if you keep mine."

"I don't have one, not really," Shelby denies.

I roll my eyes. "You're a terrible liar." Nodding to the door, I take another look around her room as I walk behind her. "You should see a doctor about that."

Shelby's face scrunchies. "Are all brothers this annoying? I'm suddenly very grateful I'm an only child."

I laugh when she shoves me in front of her.

"How was the party?" I ask, leading her to the living room.

Shelby stumbles into my back.

"Woman, have you been drinking?" I laugh, turning to help her straighten.

She gives a sheepish look. "The party was okay. Nothing special." She waves it off, walking past me.

Now, why do I not believe that?

"What were you packing a bag for?" I ask.

Shelby sighs, closing the door behind us. I watch as she locks it, pushing the handle several times after to check and then looks up at me. "It's complicated."

CHAPTER NINETEEN

Samantha

Men, I hate them. No, I hate him.

I glare at Kaleb as he holds the diner door open for Shelby, then waits for a couple to leave before entering himself. A few of the women in the diner turn and watch him. Why does he have to be so polite and charming? *No, not charming. He's arrogant and annoying,* I amend, watching him wink at Judy.

"Hi, baby," he greets me, leaning down to kiss my right cheek.

I pull back before he can make contact.

Has he lost his fucking mind?

The look I give him asks as much. He stays bent toward me; his right hand braced on the back of my booth, his left on the table.

Annoyance washes over his features, but it fades a second later, his usual smile replacing it.

"Scooch over," he orders, his body invading my space even more.

Shuffling over, I glare at Shelby.

"Who can say no to that face?" she asks, motioning across the table to Kaleb.

I roll my eyes.

"I've been trying to talk to you," Kaleb says quietly, his body turned toward me, our knees touching.

I feel it as if his hand was resting there. The thought just makes me madder. "I haven't had my phone on me."

"All week?"

I shrug, looking away. Anywhere but at him.

The diner's owner comes to the table before I can sulk anymore.

"I thought you were out of town again," Judy says, looking at Kaleb.

"He was," I mutter dryly.

"And now I'm not." He smiles cheerfully.

Judy looks between everyone at the table. "You want the usual order?"

"I'm suddenly not hungry." I shake my head.

Kaleb tuts. "You need to eat."

"I'm not hungry," I snap.

Why does he make me so mad?

This past week has been quiet and peaceful. Boring and sad. Lonely. The fact that I missed the asshole raises my temperature more than sitting next to him does.

Kaleb leans his head back on the booth and groans. A rush of images floods my brain. What we did that night. The way he gripped my hips, the grunts he made.

I feel my face flush, heat searing through me. My chest feels tight.

I fucked him.

I had sex with Kaleb.

Guilt, disgust, embarrassment, and shame consume me. But it's what I don't feel that tips me over the edge. Regret.

"Samantha," Kaleb whispers. His hand feels heavy and intrusive on my thigh, and even though it's under the table, I feel exposed.

Do they know?

I spin my head, looking around, but the only people staring are Kaleb, Shelby, and poor Judy. The older woman probably thinks I've lost my damn mind.

"Move," I practically shout, shoving Kaleb in the side.

"Sam," he tries, but I'm done. I need to leave. "Samantha," he says again in a tone I recognize as my last warning.

Stop now, or I'll have a red ass.

If I wasn't in the middle of a breakdown, I'd listen, but I am, so instead, I shuffle toward the end of the bench, pushing my body against his.

The fucker barely moves. I hate him more.

"Sorry about that." Kaleb smiles at Judy like I'm not making a scene. He reaches for his wallet.

Judy waves him off when he tries to pass her two fifties.

"For today and last week," he explains.

Closing my eyes, I count to ten and take a deep breath. I feel a buildup behind my eyelids, and I need to get out of here before they come.

"You had three orders of waffles."

"I hear that granddaughter of yours is having braces fitted next month." I feel him shrug.

"Sooner," Judy chats. "She's not looking forward to it, a little self-conscious."

"She's at that age. They'll be off before she knows it."

I hear Judy agree before someone calls out from another table.

"I owe you a meal, Shelbs."

"It's okay," my best friend replies, her voice wavering. Even she thinks I've lost it.

I feel her eyes on me. What is she thinking? A few days after Kaleb left last week, I panicked and told her everything. She sat and listened. Never judged, at least not out loud. She even made sure I got home safe after I drank a bottle of wine alone.

But I haven't seen her since. She's been busy. *Or she thinks you're a freak who fucked her own brother.*

He's not my brother!

The first tear makes its escape.

Kaleb's hand slides along my lower back to my right hip, where it stays.

"Come on," he urges softly, encouraging me out of the booth after him.

My body shivers at the touch, igniting. My heart pounds in my chest, matching the pulse in my clit.

Another tear spills.

Kaleb keeps his hand anchored, leading me out to the parking lot.

"My car's over here."

His words are a mental slap, and I stagger away from him.

"I'm not going anywhere with you." I shake my head. "I lied." I sniffle. "Earlier," I explain, wiping the back of my hand under my nose. My voice is thick with tears. "I had my phone, and I just didn't want to talk to you. Ignoring thirty calls should have been a clue," I say, my voice raising. "Stop calling, and stop texting. Leave me the fuck alone, Kaleb."

I hate myself, and he should hate me too.

CHAPTER TWENTY

Kaleb

Well, that didn't go as planned.

I run a hand through my blond hair as I watch my girl storm off, grateful when Shelby all but wrestles the car keys out of Sam's hand.

Angry Samantha, plus a car never equals a good idea.

I really did fuck up with her driving lessons.

My heart shreds when I see her shoulders shake the minute she climbs into the car. Body-wrenching sobs.

How the fuck am I going to fix this? *She'll get used to it.*

Waiting to see her car pull off the lot safely, I hear my name being called somewhere behind me.

"Kaleb. I thought that was you."

Dad?

Turning, I greet him with a smile that even I think looks fake. "Hey."

He joins me in front of the diner.

"What's wrong?"

"Nothing." I shake my head.

"You can tell me anything. You know that, right?"

This time, my smile is genuine. "I know."

But I won't. I enjoy chasing and killing prostitutes, oh and I fucked your daughter are really things you never bring up. Ever.

Instead, I motion to the building behind us. "You here to eat?"

"Actually, I was looking for you. I asked Pauline to call me the minute you got back."

Does he know? No, he'd have beaten my ass by now if he did.

"Oh?"

"Listen, kiddo . . ." He looks around uncomfortably, running a hand through his graying hair. "I meant what I said. You can tell me anything."

Where is this going?

"Walk me to my car?" he asks but starts moving before I can answer.

"Dad," I urge as we get farther away from the diner, "you're freaking me out."

He stops short.

"I know, Kaleb."

My heart stops.

"Dad . . ." What the fuck am I supposed to say? I love her?

"Why didn't you tell me? No, it doesn't matter now." He shakes off the question. "How bad is it? Whatever it is, we'll fight it as a family."

I stare at him blankly; my heart starts beating for the first time in minutes. "What the fuck are you talking about?"

"The doctor, Kaleb. I mean, did you really think I wouldn't notice? At first, I thought you used your company card to tell your mother and me without telling us, you know?"

No.

"But then the accounting team mentioned your cards were stolen. You used the company card because you had to. Would you have ever told us you've been seeing a doctor out of town?"

"What?"

"Dr. Brown. The bill came through."

Oh!

I sigh in relief. "It was nothing, just a checkup." I wave it off.

"A checkup out of town?" Dad sighs, blinking quickly.

Oh shit.

"Okay." He nods, but he doesn't believe me.

"Dad, I'm okay."

He nods again.

Meeting his gaze, I promise, "I'm okay."

Dad's eyes soften, and he steps forward to cup my cheeks. "I'm sorry to pry. I just saw the nineteen grand charge and thought the worst."

"Nineteen grand?" I practically shriek.

Fucking hell, no wonder he didn't believe me. Probably thought I was dying.

Stepping back, he leans against his car.

"I was out of town and needed a consultation. There's nothing to be worried about." Not a complete lie. "Except maybe the price of medical care in this country," I joke. Nineteen grand? Greedy little fucker.

I feel guilty keeping the truth to myself, but my birth mother isn't someone I want to share with the Cromwells. I won't let her ruin that part of my life.

"No medication?" he asks.

I shake my head.

"Nope, and no follow-up."

"You look tired," he observes.

"I am." I sigh, leaning on his car beside him, shoulder to shoulder. Just thinking about the last two occasions I've spoken to Samantha deflates me.

She's not going to make this easy for me. *You wouldn't enjoy it if she did.*

"I could sleep for a week," I mutter into my hands as I scrub my face. Digging the heel into my eyes, I sigh again.

I really am tired. Tired of running from what I feel, tired of fighting it, tired of not having what I want most in this world.

"So do it."

My eyes spring open at his words. Did I say it out loud?

"Go to the cabin. No work, no stress. Relax and just do whatever you want. I'll send out a family text. No one will go there. You'll be by yourself. Sleep until your body is rested."

I open my mouth to argue.

"No," he interrupts, holding up a finger. "I'm not asking. I'm telling. I'd say two weeks, but your mom will probably give you a week, ten days tops."

I laugh because it's true. Helen Cromwell likes her babies close.

"Daniel and Charlie will be home with the baby."

"They'll understand. Besides, you can do what you want, go where you want, see who you want. But that cabin will be a no-go zone for at least seven days. I want you healthy and happy, Kaleb. If that means having time to yourself, then so be it."

"Work—"

"Can manage," he interrupts. "You work more shifts than anyone there, but we have new hires and plenty of drivers. I'd rather lose contracts than lose my son."

His words fill me with love. I couldn't have asked for a better family or a better father.

Pushing off the car, I hug him. His arms instantly wrap around me.

"I love you," I breathe.

Christopher holds me tighter. "I love you too, kiddo."

I pat his back and try to step away, but he hugs me for a few more seconds.

"You're really okay?" he asks, releasing me.

"I am. Nothing rest and a mini staycation won't fix."

"Good." He smiles.

"Can you ask Lara to keep sending me daily pictures of the baby, please? And will you tell me when Daniel and Charlie are home, and I'll come over? I don't want to miss it."

"Of course. You won't miss anything," he promises.

I go to leave, but Dad hesitates while opening his car door.

"I know what happened at your house last week with the burglary probably added to the stress and your health. Is it wrong of me to be thankful that you were there to protect your sister?"

"No." I shake my head. "I'm glad I was there too."

"I'll never be able to thank you enough for that, Kaleb. Take as long as you need. I'll make sure no one bothers you. Except your mother. After about a week, she'll hunt you down. Like a lion with her cubs, that one."

"You love her for it."

"One of many things I love about her," he agrees.

I want that. I want someone to love me for who I am. My strengths, my flaws, all of it. Not just anyone, I want Samantha to love me that way.

How am I supposed to do that when she won't even talk to me?

CHAPTER TWENTY-ONE

Kaleb

Sighing so hard my lips move, I throw the television remote down to the other end of the sofa, past my feet.

I'm bored.

The cabin is quiet, too quiet. True to his word, Dad made it clear to everyone that I was to be left alone. He's also confiscated my office key and ordered Pauline to ignore me.

No jobs, no stress. *It's fucking killing me.*

Two days with nothing to do but think about Sam. All it's done is frustrate me more.

Horny and lonely. Not a great combination.

I sigh again. I can't sit around here much longer. My fingers itch to text or call Samantha but I haven't reached out to her since she told me to stop. That's also killing me.

Fuck it. I need to get out. Out of the house and out of my own head.

Daniel and Charlie came back today, Michael and Lara too. The whole family is back in Cromwell. And while I know they would welcome me with open arms for the night, I don't want to bother them with my mood.

Michael has his wife to himself for the first time in days. Daniel and Charlie are staying with my parents for the week so Charlie has more help to rest and recover. A newborn and a toddler are a handful, and our parents are more than happy to help.

But after spending three hours on a video call earlier, I could see that they all needed to rest.

So the local bar it is.

There will be someone I know there, which is one of the advantages of living in a small town. Everyone knows everyone.

CHAPTER TWENTY-TWO

Samantha

Scratching my nail on the tabletop, I glance around the room.

Why the fuck am I here?

The bar is full and loud, but that's what I need. What I don't need is handsy Jasper joining me at my table.

I roll my eyes at the nickname. The man can't help himself. His clammy hand lands on mine, making me cringe. He really does have a problem.

The house is too crowded with my brothers and their families there. I love my family, I do. But five adults and two children are too much, at least when I'm in this mood.

Sliding my hand from beneath Jasper's, I tilt my phone toward me. Nothing. No missed calls or texts.

Kaleb hasn't reached out once since I last saw him.

Because you went psycho and scared him off.

For the millionth time since Dad told us the cabin was off-limits, I think about calling Kaleb. Dad said he's okay, but I'd rather hear it for myself. No, I'd rather see it for myself.

"You wanna get out of here?"

I look at Jasper like he has three heads. *What are people in this town smoking?*

"No," I say, shaking my head with a scrunched face.

"I think that's enough for you, Jasper."

Jasper and I look behind him where Kyle Cooper stands with his hand clamped on Jasper's shoulder.

"You're not a cop anymore, Cooper, so fuck off. She's sitting in a bar alone; she wants to go home with someone."

Gross.

"Or she wanted a drink."

"Or that," I agree, toasting my mostly empty glass toward Cooper.

"Take a hike, Jasper."

"The lady and I were talking." Jasper huffs.

"Really? Because to me, it looked like you sat with her, and she was ignoring you."

Jasper looks between us but eventually gets up, knocking into the chair next to him. Sloppy and drunk.

"Thanks." I smile at Cooper.

"Don't thank me yet," he replies, holding his arm high to get the server's attention. Once he has it, Cooper signals that we want two more beers.

He sits in Jasper's vacated seat; an awkward silence settles.

"How have you been?" I ask.

"Better," he answers, his eyes watching the server.

"I'm sorry about you losing your job."

Cooper shrugs. "It's been a few years. I'm over it."

"We haven't exactly spoken since."

I feel him before I see him. Goose pimples spread over my body, my nipples bead, and the hair on the nape of my neck tingles.

Kaleb's here.

My eyes drift around the bar. He's at the doorway, and he's furious.

I look behind me to see what he's glaring at, but it's just the usual—people drinking, dancing, and being too much.

I turn back to face Kaleb.

He's walking toward me. My chest rises and falls quickly, my little black dress suddenly feeling restrictive and tight on my chest.

Where has all the air gone?

Kyle sneers when Kaleb comes to a stop next to our table. But he doesn't look at Cooper. His eyes haven't left me.

Of all the shit I've pulled over the years, Kaleb has never looked at me with such rage. Not even when I totaled his car.

Normally, I'd enjoy seeing him this riled, and thrive in having his full attention, but I don't feel the usual satisfaction. Mainly because I don't know what I did wrong.

"You have to be fucking joking."

I look around again just to be sure he's talking to me. Yep.

"Have you lost your fucking mind?" Kaleb hisses.

"Hey, now. The lady can do what she wants," Cooper states, starting to stand from his chair.

That gets Kaleb's attention.

"Sit back down before I make you."

People from nearby tables have started to look, and my earlier confusion is replaced by embarrassment and anxiety.

"Kaleb . . ." I start.

"Not a fucking word," he orders; his finger held up to me.

"We were just having a drink." Cooper smirks. His face changes just for a second, but I see it. No longer the sweet guy coming to the rescue, he's enjoying this. Kaleb's anger is what he wants.

I open my mouth to reassure Kaleb that nothing was going on, but before I can, he takes a step toward me, bending his large body until his shoulder is at my stomach and then bounds an arm around my thighs.

I give a startled scream as I'm thrown over his shoulder.

A cheer goes through the bar.

Can you die from embarrassment?

I don't fight him for fear of causing even more of a scene. Instead, I feel tears build as we leave the building. Humiliated.

I am never speaking to Kaleb again. *Asshole.*

My body slides against his as he lowers me. It takes everything I have not to kick him in the balls.

"Of all the men in this town." He shakes his head. "That man hates us, and you're out here trying to fuck him. Get in the car, Samantha."

"I went for a drink, Jasper sat at the table, and Kyle came over to help. He was being nice. Something you'd know absolutely nothing about."

Dropping into the passenger seat, I reach for the door handle and slam the door before he can stop me.

Kaleb closes his eyes, tilting his face toward the sky. It looks like he's trying to calm himself, like I'm not the injured party here. What's he got to be mad about, other than being such a dick?

As he rounds the car, I see Cooper standing at the bar door watching us.

The inside of the car stays silent as we head out of the lot.

"You really think he did that to be kind? We got him fired!" he reminds me.

"I didn't," I stress, poking my chest.

"Fine. Daniel, Dad, Michael, and I are the reason that asshole isn't a cop anymore. He fucking hates us. And by us, I do mean you as well," he clarifies.

He's right. I know he is, I saw Cooper's face, but

after that exit, every fiber of my being tells me to argue and not let him win.

"Who I have drinks with is not your business."

"The fuck it's not," he argues, taking his eyes off the road to glance at me. "Everything you do is my business, Samantha."

"Do you have any idea what you just did back there?" I ask, pointing back in the direction of the bar.

"Yes." He nods. "I stopped you from fucking the one guy in this town that needs stabbing."

Shock rolls through me at his words.

"How can you say that? After everything that happened at your house?"

Kaleb sighs, wiping a hand over his exhausted face.

My dad's words of Kaleb going to the cabin to rest ricochet in my head.

"Here I am, fighting with myself about letting you have the space you need and just taking the reins like you obviously need me to, and you're out here trying to fuck the closest loser."

"You're a dick, you know that?" I ask, my voice thick with emotion. Instead of backing down, I hit back. "Who I fuck is none of your concern either."

"Seeing as my cum was dripping out of that pretty pussy of yours not that long ago, I think it is my concern."

My heart stops at his words.

"Stop the car."

"Sam," he sighs.

But I don't want to hear it.

"Stop the fucking car!" I scream.

I need to be away from him. Now. Throwing the car door open, I jolt forward when the car screeches to a halt. Thank God for seat belts.

"Woman, you're fucking crazy!"

No, you just drive me mad!

Releasing the belt, I practically fall out of the car. I don't respond. I don't even look back at him. I just leave the passenger door wide open and run.

We're only a few streets away from the house, so I cut through a few yards and don't stop until I'm safely away from him. Tears stream down my face.

I hate him.

I hate me.

I hate us.

CHAPTER TWENTY-THREE

Kaleb

It's gone. My patience with her is done.

If Samantha wants to act like a brat, I'll treat her like one. At this point, the question is which does she need more: a good spanking or a good hard fuck.

Throwing the back door open, I storm through the laundry room until the door to the back stairs is suddenly blocked.

Daniel. The man is an unmovable tank. My oldest brother stares at me unmoving. Arms crossed against his huge chest, he widens his stance.

Samantha, I can strong-arm into listening to me. Daniel, not so much.

"This is between her and I, big guy."

"She's crying," he says.

"I had noticed," I snap back. "Grrr." I scrub my face. Anger won't get me anywhere with him.

"What's going on here?"

We both turn to Charlie as she steps into the laundry room.

"Hi," I breathe, bending to kiss her cheek. "You should be resting. Are you even allowed to be walking around?" I ask, but my eyes direct the question to my brother.

"She shouldn't be," her husband agrees.

"The baby is sleeping." She shrugs. "I heard the door open. I can't sit for twenty-four seven."

Daniel turns to her. "I'll take twenty-three hours of the day then."

Charlie chuckles at his words. "Kiss me," she demands.

I look away when my brother ducks to press his lips to hers.

"Now, what's going on with you?" Charlie grills me.

"Sam and I are arguing," I explain.

"Oh, she's in the kitchen."

"Charlie." Daniel frowns.

Unbothered by her husband, Charlie shrugs. "They need to work it out at some point."

At least someone's trying to help me.

I look between the couple. "I'll fix this. I'll take her to the cabin, and we'll talk it out."

Daniel remains quiet for a few minutes before giving a short nod. "Mom and Dad are upstairs. As are my children. She goes quietly and willingly," he informs, permitting me, but I hear the warning.

"I would never hurt her," I state. Needing him to hear it.

He knows; it's written all over his face.

"Everyone knows that, silly," my sister-in-law soothes, rubbing my arm.

"I caught her with Cooper," I blurt.

Daniel's head snaps to me, but I don't elaborate. They'll give me more time with her if they think she needs a good talking-to.

My brother steps forward to kiss his wife's head, then motions for me to follow him. We head straight for the kitchen, where my girl sits at the kitchen island holding a cup of cocoa.

"We're leaving," I tell her.

"You can do whatever the fuck you want, but I'm staying here."

Her eyes are red, and her cheeks still wet. My heart crumbles seeing her hurt, but we need to work this out. We can't keep going like this.

"I wasn't asking. You're going to get your ass in my car, and we're going to go sort this out. I'm done, Sam. Enough."

"Mom and Dad are upstairs," she challenges.

"Great." I smile. "Let's go have a chat with them," I bluff.

Her face drops. That's what I thought.

"Get your ass in the car. Now."

The hot chocolate sloshes over the rim of the cup and onto the marble counter.

"Fine. You wanna fight this out? Let's fight it out," she hisses, moving past me.

"I'm not fighting. I told you I was done."

She blinks quickly at my words but continues moving to the back door.

"Sorry to bother you both." I apologize to the couple who are still watching.

"You're coming over for dinner on Thursday? Meet the baby in person," Daniel asks.

"Of course." I nod. My eyes drift to the stairs.

"I dare you," Charlie challenges, knowing I'm tempted to sneak up for a quick snuggle. "If you even think about going in the room, he wakes up. He is not a deep sleeper."

"You can hold him Thursday. Come at four, and you can get an hour of cuddle time in before Michael gets here and steals him away," Daniel offers.

"Give him and Belle a kiss for me. We'll be back in a couple of days."

"Samantha is staying with you until then?" Daniel asks.

"Yes."

Whether she likes it or not.

CHAPTER TWENTY-FOUR

Samantha

I'm shaking with rage when Kaleb slides into the driver's seat.

"I can't believe you said that," I cry, referring to his earlier words and why I fled the car.

"What are you mad about, Sam? What I said or that it's true?"

Both.

Turning off the road, Kaleb drives us toward the cabin.

"We had sex," he says candidly.

I shake my head, my tears coming fast.

"Say it!" he demands.

"No," I whimper.

"What did I do, Samantha? What did you let me do? Hmm?" he asks, his tone mocking.

"Stop it!" I shout.

"No," he refuses, "I want you to say it. Maybe then you'll stop pretending it never fucking happened."

"I can't," I cry.

"Say it!"

"No!"

"Say it!"

"We had sex!" I scream. "You fucked me. Are you happy now?" I sob.

"I'm not your brother, Samantha. I'm not."

"You are," I argue. Tears and snot mix. I hiccup, trying to drag in more air.

"Deep breaths," Kaleb coaches, his hand gripping the back of my neck. "Easy, baby."

I shove his arm away. "This is what you wanted, isn't it?"

Kaleb looks over, bewildered. "You think I want you sobbing in my car? This is killing me, Samantha. I don't want you hurting. I just want you. I want us to be happy."

"Happy?" My laugh sounds hollow. "You think fucking my brother makes me happy?"

"I am not your brother!" he roars, looking away from the road.

"But that's what everyone thinks. It's what people will say."

"Who gives a fuck?"

"I do!" I scream, stabbing a finger into my chest. "People will talk, Kaleb. Mom and Dad . . ." I'm unable to finish the thought aloud.

"Mom and Dad will not walk away from you. No matter what, you won't lose the family," he promises.

"What about you? You're my best friend. What if this ends badly? We can't go back." I gulp air, my tears finally slowing.

"If this ends?" Kaleb repeats. "It's not ending, Samantha," he states like it's a matter of fact, his voice taking on an authoritative tone that's usually followed up with a spanking. "I'm done fighting."

Why do those words make me want to cry again?

I huff out a breath and wipe my face. "You'll find someone else, Kaleb. You're funny and sweet. Stern but soft. Any woman will be lucky to have you," I whisper, barely able to get the last few words out.

His gaze keeps flicking from the road to me.

"And so will I. I'll marry a sweet guy from out of town, someone who can look at me the way Daniel looks at Charlie, without everyone losing their minds because he will have no connection to this family." The words leave a sour taste in my mouth. I don't want some dope from out of town. I want Kaleb.

"The fuck we will." Kaleb chuckles, but it sounds bitter and mean. "Nothing is perfect, Sam. Not even those two. You wanna be like them? Fine. I'll show you exactly how our brother got that wife of his."

My brows furrow. Before I can ask what he means, his large hand releases my seat belt, then grips the back of my neck.

His left hand drops to his lap, unbuttoning and

unzipping his jeans. His knees steady the steering wheel.

"What the fuck are you doing?" I screech.

"Giving us exactly what we both need."

His cock is hard and leaking as he frees it from his pants. He's large and thick.

My body clenches, remembering the feel of him inside me.

"We can't," I resist, trying to pull away, but his hold stays firm, lowering my head into his lap.

"We are. You are."

His left hand returns to the wheel while his right holds me over his shaft. I watch as it twitches with every puff of my breath.

Kaleb may not be able to see it, but my body is just as aroused as his.

"Suck, Samantha."

Despite my earlier words, I want this just as much as he does, so I do as I'm told.

I stop fighting myself, turn off my brain, and just give in.

"Ahhh." His cry of pleasure echoes through the small space when my mouth engulfs him.

I don't give him time to adjust. Hollowing my cheeks, I suck. I make shallow movements at first, but the hand on my nape is heavy and insistent, forcing my mouth farther down his erection.

The wide tip hits the back of my throat. Gags mix with groans. His fingers twist in my hair, the pain only adding to my own arousal.

Moaning, I suck harder.

Kaleb releases my hair. His hand trails down my back and over my ass, where he gives me a solid smack. The thin dress does nothing to shield the force of it.

My cry of outrage is muffled and useless as he does it again.

"Faster, baby. I'm just turning onto Ellis Road."

We're nearly at the turn for the cabin's road. I wiggle my hips, desperate for friction, anything to help with the pulsing of my clit.

His words and voice just remind me of who we are and what we're doing. Tears spill out onto my cheeks, rolling down until they drip off my top lip and onto his cock. My mouth wipes them away as I swallow him again, like they were never there.

My head bobs over and over.

"Fuck, fuck, fuck," Kaleb chants above me.

I try to slide my hand up the front over my dress, but Kaleb spanks my ass again.

"Don't even think about it. Focus on me," he orders, but his actions soften his words. The hand on my ass moves farther down the curve of my ass. He pulls up my dress, and his hand disappears between my legs. Quick, hurried rubs have me on the edge in seconds.

I'm going to come.

My head rises, leaving his cock wet and angry in the night air. My jaw aches. "Ahh," I cry out so close to release.

His hand disappears.

"Finish me. Wrap those pretty lips around my dick, and don't even think about spitting. I wanna see it in your mouth," he growls.

Strong fingers once again press through my panties. They're soaked. Useless, they sit in the way of what I really need—his fingers buried deep inside me.

Kaleb's groaning picks up, and his chest rises quicker and quicker above me. His cum shoots to the back of my throat at the same time the car picks up speed.

Not wanting his movements between my legs to stop, I swallow him down, sucking out everything he has to give.

My mouth opens with a cry, my orgasm a rub or two away. His cock leaves my mouth with strings of spit and cum connecting us.

His right hand leaves me, denying my release. Tangling in my hair, he arches my head back until I'm looking at him.

Kaleb's forehead is covered in sweat, his chest heaving. Driving the car straight, he looks down his nose, keeping his eyes on me and his head tilted back into the headrest.

Close by, large trees pass us quickly outside the window. We're on our private road.

The car jerks to a halt, and my hands grip his thigh to keep myself from falling, but I shouldn't have worried. Releasing my hair, Kaleb moves his hand to the right side of my ribs, keeping me planted where I am.

His cock bobs, still just as hard as before.

"Open your mouth."

Knowing what he'll see, I do as I'm told. I can still taste him and feel strings of his cum on my chin and lower lip. My cheeks pull where my tears have dried. I'm a mess.

Gray eyes zero in on my swollen red lips. The heat in them doubles.

"Now, I'm going to show you how I get my women."

What?

I blink up at him.

His left hand appears in front of my face. I watch as his pointer finger moves to tap the glass, pointing at the woods on the other side of the window.

"Run."

Shaking my head, I push up off his thigh, moving to kneel in the passenger seat.

"Kaleb." I sigh.

His right thumb traces over my abused lower lip.

"You're going to get out of this car, go into those woods, and run."

"No, I'm not," I say, like he's lost his mind.

"Yes, you are." He nods. "When I find you, and I will, I'm going to fuck you hard enough that you never forget what we are."

I swallow hard.

Blinking, I stare at him for a second. "And if I don't?"

He gives another careless shrug. "The hood of this car looks as good a place to fuck you. But you won't be coming anytime soon."

I gulp at the look he's giving me.

My breasts feel heavy, and the coil in my belly starts anew.

How do you say no to something like that?

You don't.

CHAPTER TWENTY-FIVE

Kaleb

Excitement and arousal tangle in my stomach.

All the years that I've fantasized about this, imagining that it was Samantha I was chasing through the woods, I never thought it would happen.

I never thought we'd get here, that she and I were a possibility.

We need to talk about a lot of things, work out our differences, and come to an agreement that we're both happy with, but one thing that's not up for debate is us. Samantha is mine, and she's about to discover what that truly means.

I can barely get my cock back in my pants I'm so hard. Just seeing my girl walking to the woods with hesitant steps, glancing back at me every few seconds, has me on the edge of coming again.

Her short dress has been pulled back down, but it rides with her movement, barely covering her ass.

Sam stands on the forest edge, watching as I walk to the back of my car. Popping the trunk, I move the carpet back and reach into the hidden section of the floor.

The white of my mask practically glows in the dark.

My body is primed and ready for what is about to come . . . the chase of a lifetime.

CHAPTER TWENTY-SIX

Samantha

The beating of my heart is so loud that Kaleb can probably hear it, even at this distance.

My legs tremble. What the fuck are we doing? I'm standing opposite our family's cabin with a man the world sees as my brother, his taste still in my mouth.

I lick my swollen lips. I don't think I'll ever forget his taste.

Clouds of cold air collect in front of my face, but I don't feel the bite of the night. My body is still ignited from what we did in the car.

I frown, watching Kaleb mess in the trunk.

His eyes meet mine, and my heart stops. The loving, playful man I know disappears in an instant. A darkness washes over and settles on his face before he slides a white hockey mask over his head.

What is he doing? I thought the scarecrow masks that appear all over town on Halloween were creepy, but this one makes my skin crawl.

Kaleb takes a step in my direction.

Fuck! Fuck! Fuck!

My feet move on their own, stepping backward away from the soulless gray eyes watching me.

I don't know who this is, but it isn't my Kaleb. I look at the house on the other side of the car. He'd catch me before I even made it to the door.

So I do the only thing I can.

I do what he wants.

I turn and run.

Tree branches block my way, forcing me to duck and weave. The wind attacks my face, arms, and legs, but I'm almost too hot to really care. My ankle slips, causing me to hiss. These shoes were not made to run in!

My pulse beats strongly in every part of my body; my fast-pumping legs, my throat, my ears but nothing compares to the way my clit pulses.

With fear and uncertainty fueling my body, I have never been more aware of my nether regions.

Giving Kaleb pleasure left me wet, but I can feel excitement drip from my core as I bend to hoist myself over a thick, bent branch.

Spinning back, I expect to see him chasing me, but I don't. Skidding to a stop, I gulp in air, enjoying the burn it brings. The roar in my ears blocks out all other sounds. My hair whips while I frantically look for him. Then I see it, a flash of white in the darkness.

Images of what will happen when he catches me excite and terrify me. My body is made up of equal parts wanting to be caught and wanting to outrun him until we both come to our senses.

Flight wins.

Pivoting to the left, I head to the water. The trees thin out quickly. The large lake reflects the moon, lighting up the area. *Better than a dark forest.*

Rushing forward, I jump down the soil bank. Losing my balance, I land on my hands and knees. Throwing myself into the bank of soil, I duck down. The water's edge moves just a few feet away.

I press myself against the bank, hiding me from view as I hear twigs snap above me. My breaths sound obnoxiously loud, a beacon to my position. My hands shake as I cover my mouth.

My knees are jelly, and my whole body trembles in anticipation.

I expect him to call out and taunt me, but Kaleb hunts me in silence. The soil near my head crumbles down.

He's above me.

My eyes widen, and my stomach drops. He won't do anything bad, right? This is Kaleb.

A deep chuckle echoes in the night.

I hear him jump down behind me, then feel the sand under my feet sink with the added weight.

Wide-eyed, I turn to face him head-on, but the

gray eyes glaring down are those of a stranger. *This may be Kaleb, but he's not my Kaleb,* I remind myself.

I scream as he reaches for me. Spinning, I bolt forward, the soft sand crumbles beneath my wedges, slowing me down.

Falling forward, I claw my fingers into the ground and push myself up, propelling farther along the shore.

I barely have my balance back when a huge body slams into me from behind. The weight and force send us both into the shallow water.

My body splays as we land.

Freezing-cold water surrounds me as his weight pushes me under.

Kaleb yanks me out with a hand gripping the back of my dress. I gasp for air. My hair flies around with the force of being lifted, and the drenched strands whip me in the face, heavy with water.

My body plunges into the water again. The hand on my back holds me down as I fight. I slap the surface of the water, kicking out my legs.

He's going to kill me!

I manage to make contact and hear him grunt. The hold on me disappears long enough for me to gasp for air. Pushing up with what little strength I have, I run, wading through the water.

Heavy waves push at my side, helping me leave.

With the dock in sight, I give my all.

Changing my direction, I head straight for the

shore rather than diagonal. I try to leave the water, but I'm not quick enough.

Kaleb is on me in seconds.

"We aren't finished," he hisses in my ear, pulling my head back against his shoulder.

His right hand roams up the front of my body, the soaked dress doing nothing to hide me. It's practically a second skin at this point.

Kaleb's fingers are harsh and rough as he squeezes my breast.

My whimper of pain makes him chuckle. The hand in my hair drops to my waist.

He easily lifts me, my back into his chest. I expect him to carry me toward the house, but he doesn't. Pivoting left, he heads deeper into the freezing-cold lake.

I land with a splash as he throws me into the shoulder-height water. Cold liquid floods my nose and mouth.

My eyes burn. Kaleb's large, blurry body wades toward me. Half his chest is still out in the night air. His blue shirt is now deep in color and stuck to him like glue.

The coldness zaps my body of all energy, and I begin to sink back below the water. Coughing, I suck in air desperately as I'm pulled to the surface. He moves me as if I weight nothing, positioning me how he wants.

I'm completely at his mercy.

Face down in the water, I struggle to break free.

Strong fingers tug my panties down to mid-thigh. My chest burns, begging for air. My dress is pushed up over my hips.

I open my mouth in a scream as he rams his cock inside me. One harsh thrust and he fills my body—no warning, no foreplay.

That chase was our foreplay, and we both know it.

Kaleb pulls my head above the surface long enough for me to suck in a few breaths. His hips are relentless and brutal in their attack.

I love every bit of it.

My inner muscles squeeze and grip, desperate to keep him inside.

His left hand anchors to my waist, pulling me back against him as hard as he can. His right never leaves my hair.

I'm torn between crying out for him to stop and coming, while he seems torn between fucking me or letting me live.

The idea that this could be it only spurs me on.

I drag in another lung full of air, before I'm dunked again. Only this time, he doesn't pull me up like before. My body flails with the need for oxygen.

I can't breathe.

I scream into the water. Kaleb fucks me harder. His roar of pleasure breaks through the water barrier.

Both of Kaleb's hands move to my shoulders as he pounds my pussy. An orgasm rips through me. His hips never stop as he empties himself inside me.

Throwing my head back, I gulp water and air, desperate to live.

Coughs shake my body, adding to my struggles. Spitting water out, I cough over and over.

The man behind me continues fucking me, his hips slowing until finally he's empty.

"You're fucking perfect," he pants.

I cry out as he leaves my body. Sore and exhausted, I struggle to get my feet under me.

Peering over my shoulder, I watch as he removes the mask, and my Kaleb returns.

Large hands cup my cheeks, and firm lips press soft, sweet kisses to my face.

"You're fucking perfect," he repeats softly.

I shiver, our panted breaths mix. Leaning up on my tiptoes, I hesitantly press my lips to his.

His lips spread underneath mine. Sharing a smile, I close my eyes.

All my fight is gone. My lips move against his, my tongue submitting to him.

CHAPTER TWENTY-SEVEN

Kaleb

I kick the door open gently. Moving into the bedroom, I'm careful of the tray brimming with breakfast and two cups of coffee.

"Good morning." I smile, seeing Sam awake.

Biting her lip, she pulls the sheet tighter to her chest shyly.

"A little late for that, aren't we?" I ask.

Her cheeks flush. I follow its path down her neck beneath the white cotton.

Setting our breakfast down on her lap, I lean down to press my lips to hers, tugging the sheet away from her upper body.

Groaning, I pull away.

"Hi," I whisper.

"Hi," she replies just as softly. Her lip reappears as she looks over the breakfast. "Kaleb—"

"No." I interrupt. "We're not starting today with an argument. We're gonna stay here in this house just the two of us until I have you compliant and ready to start this relationship together. No matter how many times I have to fuck you."

Sam licks her lips. "I was just going to say there's way too much food here." She points at the tray.

Dropping my ass on the bed at her feet, I grin, my eyes dropping to where her tits bounce.

"Guess we'll have to build up another appetite once we're done eating."

Reaching out, I pick up a strawberry and dip it into the maple syrup.

"No one's coming here, right?" she whispers.

I pause. "No." I shake my head. "It's just you and me."

Her chest rises in a soft sigh, her shoulders relaxing.

I glide the strawberry along her plump lip. "Open up," I order.

CHAPTER TWENTY-EIGHT

Samantha

My feet slap the wooden floor as I rush to the freezer. Movement to my left makes me jump.

I chuckle, my hand resting on my chest over my fast beating heart. *Relax, Sam.* I roll my eyes.

My reflection blinks back at me from the deck doors. Wide-eyed with ruffled hair and Kaleb's shirt hanging off one shoulder, I look thoroughly fucked. The man certainly kept his word of making me forget anything but us.

The world outside the cabin is drenched in darkness. The only thing I can see is the kitchen mirrored back at me.

Nothing exists but this cabin. We're in our little bubble where no one can see us, no one can judge, and no one can disagree.

I push away the pain of doubt.

Pulling open the freezer, I dig for our midnight snack, smirking when I wrap my hand around it.

Looking back at the stairs, I listen for movement but don't hear anything.

Grabbing a spoon, I drop down in front of the freezer, hidden behind the kitchen island. Chuckling, I go in for the first bite.

"Hmm," I moan, closing my eyes.

"I know that's not the caramel."

My eyes open to find a very serious Kaleb before me. Hands on his hips, he glares down at me.

"Samantha."

"No," I say with a mouthful of ice cream, stretching out my leg to kick away the lid with Caramel written in big red letters across the middle.

Kaleb purses his lips. "Do I believe you?" he asks himself, tapping a forefinger to his chin, his eyes in the air. His head snaps to me. "No."

My scream turns into a laugh when he lunges for my legs. Pulling my ankles, he drags me across the kitchen floor. Laying on my back, I chuckle as he moves me from in front of the freezer.

Dropping to his knees, Kaleb looms over me, his hands framing my hips. "It's rude not to share," he growls.

His tongue forces its way into my mouth, searching out all remains of caramel ice cream.

I lick my lips and give him a smirk. "Want some more?" I ask, lifting the carton between us.

At his nod, I sit up and scoop another spoonful of ice cream.

"Kaleb!" I cry out, my left hand clinging to his shoulder.

Strong hands grip my ass, lifting me into the air and on to his lap. He kneels below me, resting his ass on the heels of his feet.

The cream falls off the spoon and onto my chest between the open buttons of his shirt.

"Oops." He smirks.

Kaleb leans forward, licking it away.

"Mmm," he moans, looking up at me. "My new favorite flavor, bratty caramel."

I roll my eyes. "I am not a brat." I huff.

"No?" He smirks.

"Nope." I shake my head. "Besides, people are only bratty when they can't be handled," I challenge, resting my forearms on his shoulders.

We stare at each other, a moment passing between us. I see it in the way he looks at me, the way his gaze softens and his lips curl.

Don't say it. We can't say it.

I shake my head, urging him to keep it to himself.

Kaleb blinks, his smile leaving. And just like that, those forbidden feelings are tampered down, replaced with what we can have. Lust.

"Oh, I'm going to handle you," he growls.

CHAPTER TWENTY-NINE

Samantha

"Do I look okay?" I fret, smoothing down my jacket.

"You look perfect." Kaleb smiles.

"You're just saying that because we don't have time for me to change again."

"Yes." He nods. "But you're perfect."

I melt as his hands frame my face.

"Do I look different?" I ask against his lips.

"No." He frowns.

"Do you think they'll know?" I worry as he ushers me out the door.

"What?" He chuckles. "That we've been fucking like bunnies for the past few days."

I still at his words. This is not funny.

Kaleb holds his hands up in surrender. "No one will know."

My phone sounds inside the cabin.

Kaleb pats his pockets down. "It's not mine." He goes to take a step inside.

"Leave it," I rush, grabbing his arm.

He looks at me, confused.

"Anyone important is about to be with us," I throw out quickly.

"Could be Shelby."

"Maybe"—I shrug—"but she's been busy lately. I'm not sure what's going on with her."

"Oh, she's fine." He grins.

I raise a brow.

"She has a man," he explains, leading me to the car.

"Why do you know and I don't?" I ask offended. She's my best friend.

"Because I'm more observant. She'll tell you when she's ready."

"Do I know him?"

"My lips are sealed," Kaleb declares, miming zipping his lips and throwing away a key.

"I wish," I huff, earning a laugh and a firm squeeze to the nape of my neck.

I fidget the entire way home. Having had enough, Kaleb grabs my hand.

"Everything is going to be fine. We'll officially meet the baby, cement our positions as favorite aunt and uncle, eat, drink, and then head back to the cabin. We're going to have a good evening."

His words help me relax. Of course it's going to

be okay. It's our family.

As soon as we park, I pull my hand from his, earning a hurt look.

Cringing, I step out of the car quickly.

"There are my babies," Mom greets warmly. "I didn't expect you to arrive together."

My stomach drops, and I feel myself pale.

"I picked her up." Kaleb saves us, settling his hand on the small of my back.

"You didn't have to do that. Your dad or I could have swung by Shelby's."

Shelby's? Oh, right, that's where they think I'm staying.

"Is Shelby, okay? I worry about her, especially with her asking you to stay with her. Maybe she should move in with us permanently. That way, she won't be alone." Mom worries.

"Shelby's fine, Mom." Kaleb smiles, leaning in to kiss her cheek. "What food do I smell?"

Instantly distracted, Mom leads us into the kitchen, where most of the family waits.

"Baby," I quietly squeal, my worries and insecurities about Kaleb and me forgotten.

"Wanna hold him?" Charlie offers.

I cradle him carefully, "He's perfect. Look at that little nose." I melt. "Kaleb, do you see him?"

"I see him," he whispers. Stepping in close, he presses the front of his body against my side, his right arm wrapping around my shoulders as he peers down at our nephew. "He's beautiful. Takes after his mother of course."

"Of course," I agree like it's the most obvious statement ever.

Everyone chuckles.

"How are you doing?" Kaleb asks, moving around the kitchen to kiss Charlie's cheek.

"Exhausted."

But the look on her face says she wouldn't have it any other way.

I glance around the kitchen. "Is Belle already in bed?"

Charlie nods. "Daniel and your dad are just reading her a story. They'll be a while."

We should have come earlier.

"The dear has been a little clingy ever since the baby came home." Mom adds.

"She's just not used to sharing Daniel and me." Charlie blushes.

"Not a problem, sweetheart." Mom waves away. "Did I ever tell you about how Sammy used to cling to me in the early days of Daniel and Michael coming home?"

"Really?" Charlie smiles.

"Oh, yeah. Wouldn't leave me alone. Day and night. Still climbs in with us sometimes even now." Mom laughs.

"Okay," I huff. "Let's not tell everyone that."

"Nothing to be ashamed of, baby. Some people just like a cuddle."

"Hmm." I side-eye her. "I'm not giving this baby back tonight," I declare and head for the living room.

"No fair," Kaleb moans. "Charlie, Sam's hogging the baby."

"Snitch."

"Mom," Kaleb whines, "Sam called me a snitch."

Laughing, everyone joins us in the living room.

"We'll wait for the boys to come down for food. How about a board game?"

I drown out Michael and Kaleb bickering about what to play, and instead, I focus on the new family member.

Feeling Charlie settle beside me, I whisper, "What's his name?"

"Nope," she denies me gently. "My husband wants the pleasure of announcing that."

CHAPTER THIRTY

Kaleb

"I can't move," Samantha groans from across the room.

It feels like I haven't been near her since we got here.

Because you haven't. My bratty girl is avoiding me.

"At least you finally stopped hogging little Griffin over here," I say with a raised brow.

"Not Griffin." Daniel shakes his head at my guess, rocking his son.

"Little Roman?"

Charlie laughs. "Put them out of their misery."

My oldest brother steps toward me. "Careful," he warns, placing the baby into my arms.

As if I'd actually drop him. I fight an eye roll. I've been spending too much time with Shelby.

"We'd like you to meet Rupert Kaleb Cromwell."

My eyes instantly fill at his words. The small child blurs as I blink.

"You didn't have to," I whisper, overwhelmed.

"I don't do anything I don't want to," Daniel reminds me.

I look up at my brother. Even at my six foot one, he makes me feel small.

Slowly, I sink onto the footstool.

"What about Michael?" I ask, unable to look up at my family.

"Michael will be his godfather. Besides, he knows how I feel. Sometimes you need reminding," Daniel explains.

"Dad?" I ask, inquiring about Christopher's name.

"Rupert and Belle both carry the Cromwell name. We honor him that way. You deserve this, baby brother." He grips my shoulder.

A tear splashes, landing on Rupert's little cheek, and I quickly wipe it away.

"Hi, Rupert Kaleb." Any other words I have get lodged in my throat.

I fucking love this family. I'm not ready to lose them.

Everyone crowds around, commenting on how they love the name. No one mentions my tears or how I won't pass him off. They leave us be.

At least until the little man in my arms stretches, releasing a whimper that silences the entire room.

"Sorry, Kaleb." Charlie stands. "That's my cue.

He's due a feed." Pressing a kiss to the top of my head, she takes little Rupert back. "Free cuddles anytime you want," she offers, straightening.

"With the baby too, right?"

I don't see it coming, but I sure as fuck feel it. My head snaps forward with the smack Daniel delivers to the back of my head.

"You deserved that." Lara laughs.

"Mom, Daniel hit me."

"I didn't see anything." Mom smiles, sipping her wine. "Stop teasing your brother."

"I'll be right back." Charlie excuses herself. "I'm okay." She smiles up at her husband when he moves to follow. "You stay with your brothers, play and eat."

"I'll come with you," Sam volunteers when Daniel hesitates.

"But I wanted a rematch," I complain, gesturing to the Scrabble board.

"I don't wanna play with you. You cheater."

I clutch my chest. "Are you implying that I cheat?"

"I'm not implying anything. I'm saying it."

And because I can't help myself where she's concerned, I call out, "You love playing with me." As she follows Charlie upstairs.

Without turning, Sam discreetly throws me the middle finger.

Laughing, I turn back around in my seat.

Michael watches me with a raised brow.

"What?" I snap.

"You tell me," he challenges.

His smirk pisses me off the longer I look at it.

"How are you feeling?" Mom asks from her armchair, the glass of wine emptying quickly.

"Good." I nod.

"You look better. Relaxed. Happy," Dad adds, sitting on the arm of mom's chair.

I am happy. I just need to find a way to stay like that when shit hits the fan.

"Thank you for letting me have the cabin," I say.

CHAPTER THIRTY-ONE

Kaleb

I watch my girl fidget with the cushion in her lap. If she pulls that loose thread any harder, she's going to unravel the stitching.

Speaking of things unravelling, her eyes widen when a cell phone chimes somewhere in the kitchen.

Why is she so jumpy? Maybe it's time to go.

The sofa shifts below me, Charlie settles with the help of her husband's hand on her elbow.

"Kaleb." His gruff voice rumbles.

I look in the direction that he nods and frown. Michael is standing in the kitchen, stiff as a board, hands buried deep in his pants pocket.

Do they know? I eye the back door again. *Only one way to find out.*

Looking around the room, I try to think of an excuse to leave.

Charlie leans forward, distracting everyone by pointing out Rupert's birthmark. Whatever is happening, my sister-in-law is in on it.

Taking my cue, I slip out unnoticed.

Michael looks back toward the house when Daniel and I walk into Dad's workshop at the back of the yard.

"No one even knows we left. Too focused on that cute son of yours." I smile at Daniel. "Something he gets from his uncle, obviously."

"Obviously," Daniel agrees.

His words stop me dead. Something's wrong.

I glance between my brothers.

"I need you to remember where you are."

I don't respond to Michael's words. At my silence, the two men share a look. Michael nods, and Daniel sidesteps, putting his large body in front of the door.

Michael wets his lips. "While Charlie and Samantha were upstairs, Sam got upset. She confided something."

My eyes bulge. *Oh shit*, they do know.

"Cooper's been bothering Sam. He knows about the two of you."

I close my eyes. My heart drops into my stomach. I brace for impact, but nothing comes. Blinking, I furrow my brow. The full extent of his words registers, and any worries I had of being assaulted leave.

"Bothering. How?" I demand.

Michael clears his throat. "Texting. Taunting." He shrugs. "Seems he took some photo of the two of you at the cabin."

Rage rushes through me, roaring in my ears, drowning out most of Michael's words, the odd one filtering through.

"Crying . . . scared . . . embarrassed."

My chest heaves. It feels like I'm dragging sand through my lungs.

"I think she just needed to get it out."

My hand shakes, and violence rages in me. The need to stab so overpowering, I do the only thing that I can . . . I give in.

Wrapping my fingers around the screwdriver on the workbench, I plunge it into the plaster board covered wall. Ripping it out, I stab over and over. When that's not enough, I grab at anything and everything, launching objects around the room.

By the time I calm, I'm gasping for air.

How did this happen? And why the fuck did my girl not tell me?

"It's going to be okay, Kaleb," Michael reassures me from where he's retreated to the corner.

"It will," Daniel backs.

"We love you."

I swallow at Michael's declaration.

How?

A quick glance at their faces tells me it's true. Taking a deep breath, I count to ten. Then twenty, then thirty.

"I need to leave," I croak out.

"Don't be too harsh on her," Daniel orders, stepping aside from his post at the door. "She's scared, but she told someone."

I nod because it's true. Would I have preferred Sam had confided in me? Yes, but I'm just glad she didn't keep it to herself.

"He's got to go," I declare. I've had enough of this asshole.

"We'll talk about it tomorrow." Daniel slaps a hand on my shoulder. "Tonight, just focus on Samantha."

They're not going to disown me.

"I love you both, too," I whisper, entering the main house.

Striding into the living room, I pick up Sam's coat.

"Samantha, it's time to go." My words are short and sharp, but no matter how much I try to reel myself in, I can't.

We need to leave.

"Aww," she pouts, but it doesn't have its usual effect. It just makes me want to get her alone quicker.

"It's okay, sweetie. Sammy can just stay home tonight. You head on back to the cabin." Mom smiles, completely oblivious to my impending breakdown.

I don't know if it's the look on my face or the tension radiating off me, but Sam stands quickly. "It's getting late, anyway. I should go."

Dad frowns. "Mention moving in to Shelby. See if she's receptive to the idea."

"Sure," Sam agrees, shrugging into the coat I'm holding open.

It takes far too many hugs and kisses, but we're out the door four minutes later.

Closing the passenger door, I relax a little. I'll have her to myself soon. Rounding the car, I freeze.

My front tire is flat. My nostrils flare.

Fuck. Off.

"Everything okay, son?"

I pinch the bridge of my nose. "Tire's flat," I answer dryly.

A jingle of metal flies over the top of my car toward me. My right hand shoots up, catching the projectile before it can hit me in the face and really push me over the edge.

Unclenching my fingers, I stare down at a set of keys.

"Take my truck," Daniel's deep voice calls.

Waving my pointer finger in the general direction of the front door, I retrieve my girl from the car.

Giving a short explanation, I help Sam out of my car. "Tire's flat. We're taking Daniel's truck."

"Oh, we can change it now if you want? And by we, I mean you." She smirks.

My lips twitch with the need to kiss her. No one calms me like she does.

"Not tonight. I just want to go home."

Sam nods at my somber tone.

"Night," I call out, giving a final wave to our family.

CHAPTER THIRTY-TWO

Samantha

Kaleb throws his keys on the side table so hard I flinch.

He's been like this since he got into the truck to come back to the cabin. His car getting a flat isn't that big of a deal. I have no idea why he's so upset . . . well, not no idea. I might have caused some of this since I did avoid him at every turn tonight.

Cringing, I sigh. Might as well get this over with.

"Please don't be mad," I whisper. "You have to understand why we have to be careful. Mom and Dad can't know," I stress.

Kaleb drops to the sofa, his head in his hands.

When he finally looks up, he props his head on his entwined fingers. "Were you ever going to tell me?"

My stomach sinks. "Tell you what?"

His eyes narrow. "I am two seconds away from putting you over my knee, Samantha. I'm not in the mood for games."

I swallow the lump in my throat.

"Your phone," he demands, his hand stretched out.

Oh. Snitch.

"Did she at least wait until we left to snitch?"

"No. She told Michael the minute she had a chance."

I roll my eyes. *Of course she did.* I shouldn't have said anything, but I needed someone to know.

"Charlie was being a good sister-in-law, Samantha. Lose the attitude."

My eyes fill with tears at his tone. We haven't argued for days.

"Michael?" I ask, offering my phone.

Kaleb shrugs. "She needed him there to restrain Daniel when he found out. When he was reasonable, they called me out back," he explains, scrolling through my messages, his hand shaking the more he sees.

"So that's what it takes to calm you, our brothers?"

"No." He shakes his head. "I tore up the workshop and took out half the room before I calmed down."

My jaw drops at his words.

Kaleb looks up in time to see my stunned horror.

"She said you cried, Sam," he whispers, blinking

back his own tears. "He's not getting away with that shit."

He discards the cell on the sofa and stands. Embracing me, Kaleb kisses the top of my head. "I'm sorry," he whispers.

"What are you sorry for?" I sniffle.

"Kyle Cooper has been sending you awful fucking texts all day, and you didn't think you could tell me."

A sob breaks out of my chest. "I didn't want the week to end. I just wanted a few more days with you."

"I'm not going anywhere," he swears.

I wrap my arms around his waist and cuddle closer. "I didn't mean to lie."

"I know," he breathes.

"Those pictures were last night in the kitchen."

Kaleb nods above me. "He must have been outside with a camera pointing into the kitchen."

"Maybe I should go home," I suggest, but every fiber screams at me for even suggesting it.

"Not happening, baby. We're meeting up with Daniel and Michael tomorrow for lunch to discuss Cooper and what to do."

"Mom and Dad can't find out, not like this."

"He's being cruel to you, and it stops now. That's not up for debate."

My throat closes as the memory of getting the texts from an unknown number this morning. First, the lyrics to "Sweet Home Alabama" that I brushed off as a wrong number. Second was a link to an article on siblings who married and had kids. My heart had stopped at that. But the picture of Kaleb and I having sex on the kitchen floor last night, sticky with ice cream, had pulled my world apart.

I just wanted one more night of this before it all fell away.

"Maybe he's right?" I whisper into his chest, not daring to look up.

"There are many things between you and me, Samantha, but blood isn't one of them." Kaleb shakes his head. "That fucker . . ." He takes a deep breath. "Will get what's coming to him. And not everyone is as closed-minded as him."

"What if they are?"

"So fucking what." He shrugs, wrapping his arms tighter around me. If he pulls me any closer, we're going to merge into one being. "We have each other, and you have your family. It's enough," he vows, kissing the top of my head.

Our family, I silently correct. There's no way they will send him away.

CHAPTER THIRTY-THREE

Samantha

Cuddled on one of the sofas, we face each other, ignoring the film playing in the background. The room is bright and light.

Our morning has been spent exchanging sweet touches and soft kisses.

"There's something we should talk about."

I frown at his serious tone.

"Okay." I nod, waiting for him to continue.

His large chest expands, rubbing against mine.

"I can't have children, Sam."

"Oh." I frown. "Did you have an accident?"

"No." He smiles gently. "I'm sorry, I should have been clearer. I meant to say I won't have children. Biologically. I had a vasectomy."

I shift, throwing a leg over his right hip.

"I will give you everything you want. So if children are in the cards for you, then we'll find another way," he offers.

"Because of our relationship?" I ask, tearing up.

"No, no." He rushes, his hands soothing over my back. "No, baby. My line, my genes . . . her genes, they end with me."

Oh. Kaleb doesn't elaborate on who he means; he doesn't have to. I know his past life wasn't a good one. Not that any of my brothers talk about their pasts with me.

His right hand drops down to pat my ass. I'm not sure if it's to comfort himself or me.

I shrug at his words. "I always envisioned being the fun aunt anyway." I give a small smile and trace his lips with my finger. "But for what it's worth, I think you'd make a great dad."

"Yeah?"

"Yeah." I nod. "Stern but fair." I kiss where my finger has traced, peppering his lips with small kisses. "There are many ways to have a child, Kaleb."

"True." He nods. "We'll see what the future brings. But you'd be happy if children didn't happen for us?" he asks, watching my face for a reaction.

I trace the bridge of his nose down and back up between his beautiful gray eyes. My words are whispered into the small space between us. "I just want you."

A look settles onto Kaleb's face, the one from the kitchen a few nights ago.

Slowly, he rolls his large body onto mine, forcing me onto my back. His forearms bracket my head.

"Play with me?" he asks, his nose running along mine.

My body heats. Something tells me he's not talking about Clue. Shyly, I nod.

Desire pools in his eyes as he stares down at me for just a second. His cock hardens where he presses it against my core.

"Hide-and-seek. I'm going to give you two minutes."

"And if you find me?" I ask breathily.

Kaleb chuckles, the vibrations making my mouth form an O.

"When I find you," he corrects, "I'm going to fuck you like you're not my world. Rough." He shoves his hips into mine. "Harshly." He nips at my neck. "All-consuming," he swears, pulling the hair at the nape of my neck.

"If," I taunt.

Kaleb pushes up onto his hands, drawing back onto his knees just enough for me to slither my way from beneath him.

"Time starts now."

My mind races with the best place to hide, but Kaleb sits in the middle of the living room with his eyes closed. Anywhere downstairs is a no because he'll hear me. So I turn and run, taking the stairs two at a time.

"Don't fall!" Kaleb calls out sharply.

"Cheat!" I yell back, grinning when I see him looking at me with a worried expression.

He gives me a cheeky smile.

My two minutes aren't even up yet, and my body is already slick and waiting. But I'm not making it that easy for him.

I run up the next flight of stairs, making sure to be loud about it. Stopping halfway, I slide down the banister, cursing when I nearly slip backward. Silently, I hurry to our parents' room at the end of the first floor.

Just as I close the door, I catch a glimpse of Kaleb rushing up the stairs to this floor and continuing up the next flight. I leave the door open a crack to make sure he's gone.

Happy, I switch rooms, running across the hall to the one we've spent the last few nights in. Kaleb's bedroom.

The rumpled sheets greet me, and even hours after we got up, the room still smells like sex.

We really have been busy. I flush. My pussy pulses, more than ready for more, but my mind races at the best way to win.

"Samantha," Kaleb sings from the upper floor, his boots thudding as he steps down each stair.

Shit.

He cleared that floor quicker than I thought he would. Spinning, I look for a place to hide. The bathroom? *No.* The closet? *No.* Under the bed? I bite my lip. *Not this time.* My eyes linger on the window.

Hmm.

Shimmying the wooden frame up, I peer out. The top of the porch roof is just below. I glance back at the door, hearing him clearing the rooms on this floor now.

Fuck it.

Laughing quietly to myself, I climb out onto the roof and carefully walk to the corner of the house.

He'll never look out here.

Turning, I plant my ass on the wooden slats and crab crawl to the edge.

There's a pillar directly below me on the other side of the porch roof.

It's not the first time I've snuck out of this house.

With a grin, I turn onto my hands and knees, moving backward until my legs hang off one by one, my hands holding the edge of the roof.

I hear movement above me at the window, but I dare not look in fear of falling.

Wrapping my legs around the pillar, I slide down the short distance to the porch banister.

Hopping off, I breathe a sigh of relief. I may have snuck out that way before, but I've also fallen off that way before too. My late teens were . . . interesting.

I cockily skip to the porch stairs, but the minute my foot touches the first step, the front door flies open.

"I know you didn't just go out of that fucking window."

Oh shit!

I jump down all the steps, landing in a crouch, my hands bracing my fall. I feel like a frog. *A scared frog.*

"No! You're imagining things. Old age is getting to you!"

Probably shouldn't poke the bear, but I can't help myself when it comes to Kaleb Cromwell.

"Samantha Cromwell, you're going to have a red ass as well as a sore pussy when I'm finished with you."

I almost come at his words. Kaleb has spanked me many times over the years, but never in a way that's meant to be enjoyed. The idea of him doing it while inside me has me faltering in my attempt to hide behind Daniel's truck.

Dropping to my knees, I search for Kaleb's feet.

"You're just making this harder for yourself."

"I don't know. You look pretty hard," I sass, commenting on the tent in his sweats.

Kaleb chuckles as I crawl around the truck. Dropping lower, I try to see where he went again. I look left and right, but he's disappeared.

"Find what you're looking for?"

I scream at the sudden sound of his voice next to my ear.

With a shit-eating grin, Kaleb hauls me to my feet.

"You're in big trouble, little girl," he growls.

It's as if he presses factory reset. My mind goes blank, and I no longer control my body. I stand pressed face-first against the side of the truck while Kaleb opens the door.

My lungs remind me to breathe as he pushes me down over the bench seat. My toes can barely touch the ground, the gravel just scraping the tip of my sneakers.

Kaleb makes quick work of my sweats. I look back in time to see his join mine, bunched at our ankles.

He doesn't prep me, not that he needs to—my body is more than ready for him.

We both cry out as he pushes his way into me. Reaching out, I claw at the black seat, desperate to find any kind of perch, any sort of leverage as Kaleb's hips attack mine.

True to his words, he fucks me like I don't matter. The sound of skin hitting skin penetrates the winter air.

Hot and cold take turns rushing over my body every time he pulls away, and I'm exposed to the elements.

Pain and warmth suddenly ignite in my right ass cheek, followed by the sound of his hand connecting with my flesh. Like my brain can't register the feel until I've heard the sound.

My pussy quivers.

"Ahh," I cry out my pleasure.

"You will never do that again?" Kaleb grunts.

"What?" I cry, my mind still empty of all thoughts outside of the pounding I'm receiving.

What did I do? I blink, trying to remember, but

Kaleb hits a spot inside me that makes my mouth fall open. *Oh shit.*

My release builds in the pit of my stomach. I'm so close.

Another slap rains down.

"The window," he hisses, thrusting his hips. "You never do that again."

"I won't," I promise, desperate for him to give me what I need. I'd promise anything at this moment if it meant staying on the hill my body is climbing.

"Shit, shit, shit," Kaleb chants.

The frantic words pierce through my haze, along with a rumbling sound.

I turn my head, but I can only see the inside of the truck.

"There's a car coming. You need to come before it gets here."

What?

"No, no, no." I chant, trying to push myself up from the bench, but Kaleb's hold only gets stronger. A hand in the middle of my back presses me down. His hips get more demanding. His cock hits something inside me. "Oh God," I call. "Right there, right there."

"Come on," Kaleb coaches, "come on my cock while our parents drive down here."

Mom and Dad?

I don't know if it's his words, his brutal thrusts, or the feel of him striking my already sore ass cheek, but I cry out, my orgasm punching through me. It pulls the pleasure from his body, and his cum streams and streams into me.

I push myself to stand, and my hips are still flush with the edge of the truck seat. I look up the road to see the hood of our parents' car heading our way.

Kaleb grips my hips, still pumping his seed into me. His pleasure is never-ending. One last groan and his movements cease, his hips shoved tightly against my ass.

I love the feel of him so deep inside me. I miss him the instant he withdraws.

"How did you know it was them?" I pant, reaching for my sweats.

When he doesn't answer, I glance back to see Kaleb watching as his cum drips out of me.

"A guess." He shrugs calmly like we didn't just fuck in our brother's truck. "Hop in." He nods to the open door while pulling up his pants and tucking himself away.

I do as I'm told. The door clangs closed loudly behind me.

I grip the base of my throat and try to remember how to breathe.

They didn't see, I reassure myself. There's no way, not at that distance.

My heart is just starting to slow when a bang on the truck window makes me scream. Water hits the glass.

Kaleb's grinning face distorts through the water, my dad's soon joining him.

"What are you kids doing out here?"

"Cleaning Daniel's truck," Kaleb says like it's obvious. "I figure since he let me borrow it to get home last night, it's the least we can do."

Quick thinking.

I wait with bated breath for Dad's response.

"That's very thoughtful of you, son."

"What are you doing here?" Kaleb asks.

"We brought your car back. Besides, like your father could keep me away any longer." Mom tuts, rounding the truck.

"You changed the tire?" Kaleb asks Dad.

"I've been known to do that from time to time. I do own a trucking business," Dad sasses. I swear he's where I get it from. "I don't know what you went over, but it sliced the tire clean open."

"I didn't feel anything." Kaleb frowns. "Thank you for fixing it."

I watch as Mom pulls Kaleb into a hug. "How are you feeling?"

"Good. Relaxed." He smiles as she pats his cheek.

Lowering the window, I poke my head out.

"You missed a bit," I declare, pointing at a dry patch on the side of the truck.

"Oh, yeah," Kaleb agrees.

I see the look on his face but don't have time to react before the hose turns to me. Water hits my face, the spray fans out lighter than when he was aiming for the metal. Through the water I see his thumb covering the hole slightly to soften the blow.

My grin matches his.

"Asshole!"

"Samantha!" Mom and Dad yell.

Leaving me dripping in more ways than one, Kaleb continues to wash the truck.

My heart skips a beat, watching him smirk at our parents.

There's no way this can end well.

CHAPTER THIRTY-FOUR

Kaleb

"They already know. There's nothing to worry about. They love you," I promise, guiding Sam into Judy's diner.

The morning dragged on as we waited to meet the others, although our little game of hide-and-seek entertained us.

Sam slows as we approach the booth. "You didn't show them the photos, did you?"

"Are you joking? No, I actually like having my legs working."

"Have they threatened you?" Sam rushes. "I'll kick their asses if they did!"

The love I have for her swells because I know she means it.

"I wish I could kiss you right now," I whisper in

her ear, earning an elbow in the ribs. "I said I want to, not that I would," I grunt.

Who knew elbows were so sharp? I rub at my new injury.

"He misbehaving?" Michael asks as we step close to our siblings.

Sam doesn't answer. Instead, she looks like I hog-tied and forced her here.

Sliding into the booth on the empty side, she looks at anything but them.

"Anyone got anything to say?" I demand sharply, placing my arm on the back of the booth behind Samantha.

"No."

"No."

"Nope."

Everyone answers together.

"Can I have ice cream?" Belle asks from her dad's lap.

Sam's wet eyes slowly look around the table.

"You don't hate us?"

"Samantha." Daniel's stern voice breaks through the others' rushed reassurances.

Sam closes her eyes, refusing to look at our big brother.

"Samantha," he repeats.

I stroke my thumb on her neck, trying to give her the strength she needs.

Finally, she meets his gaze.

Neither sibling speaks, but a thousand words pass between them.

Sam nods, taking the menu that Michael offers.

I hold my hand out for one, and he scoffs. "Does it look like I work here? Get your own."

Samantha gives a snotty laugh, and just like that, the tension melts.

"Does this mean you're one babysitting team, or can I still count you separately?" Charlie asks cheekily.

"One," Sam answers, "but double the time."

I nod, grinning so hard that it hurts my cheeks when Samantha slides her hand onto my thigh under the table.

"You heard the lady," I agree.

A young girl approaches the table with a pad of paper and pen in her hands. "Welcome to Judy's. What can I get you?"

"Well, well, well, if it isn't little June bug," I greet. "I told your grandmother you'd look adorable with those braces."

June blushes at my words, hiding behind her long bangs.

I nudge whoever's foot is closest to my left shoe.

"I didn't even notice," Lara joins in.

I kick Michael under the table next.

"Not too bulky. They look great," he approves.

June's smile gets bigger and bigger.

"Thanks," she replies brightly. "What can I get you?"

"I want cake," Belle declares.

"Remember what Daddy said," Daniel coaches.

But his daughter ignores him in favor of the coloring book in front of her.

"Belle, you can have cake, but that means no milkshake."

That gets her attention.

"No," she whines.

"Cake or milkshake?" Daniel asks.

His daughter flops back against his chest on the verge of a tantrum. While the two parents calm her down, the rest of the table puts our order in.

"Lemon cheesecake, please," I order for myself.

"Oh, I think George just had the last piece. We have another full cake in the back fridge, but I think Grandma is saving it for a large group we have tomorrow."

June twists her lips, then squints at me. "I'll see what I can do," she whispers, looking around to make sure no one heard.

Just like her grandmother.

"Have you decided?" Daniel asks his daughter.

"Milkshake." She pouts, grumbling when her dad tickles her tummy.

"That's not how we ask."

"Please," she adds.

"Good girl," he praises, kissing the top of her head.

"Two strawberry milkshakes, please," Charlie orders, then looks at my brother.

"I'll have a chocolate milkshake and a plate of fries, please."

"So three strawberry milkshakes, two chocolate, one vanilla. A plate of fries and one lemon cheese-cake," June reads out, ending in a whisper.

"Is Rupert about to eat?" Michael asks, peering down at the baby cuddled close to his mother.

Charlie chuckles, nodding.

Sam and I exchange a confused look, then shrug it off.

"So what are we doing about Cooper?" I ask.

The women look between themselves.

"Nothing. He'll go away," Sam states in denial.

"He's not going anywhere." I shake my head.

My fingers twirl her ponytail, the blond hair thick and silky. I shake her hair to soften my words.

"Not on his own anyway," Michael mutters.

"Maybe we shouldn't discuss this here?" Lara interjects.

Probably not, but Sam was so nervous meeting up with our brothers that I thought a public place would be best.

"Maybe we should step outside for a minute?" I suggest.

My brothers grunt in agreement.

Rupert whimpers and instantly starts to cry.

"After we've all finished eating and drinking." Daniel changes his mind. "Can you manage?" he asks Charlie as she maneuvers the newborn out of the baby wrap. Pulling the wrap loose, she drapes it over her shoulders, concealing herself while her son eats.

"Momma," Belle whines, reaching for Charlie.

"Your brother is eating," Daniel tells her, pulling her back onto his lap.

The toddler does not like that. Big fat tears drip down her face. "Momma," she cries, reaching for Charlie again.

My heart shatters.

"Belle, Rupert needs Mommy right now. Can you help Daddy color this butterfly?"

"Nooo," she wails, shaking her head. Brown curls spiral out.

"How do you say no to that?" I whisper, ready to give the little girl anything she wants.

"He rarely does," Charlie answers.

She leans over to kiss his bicep. Pulling back the wrap, she shows her husband their baby boy. Daniel nods as if it strengthens his resolve.

"He's eating well," he praises, pressing a kiss to her forehead.

We rally around the table and manage to distract Belle long enough for her milkshake to arrive. Drinking happily, she forgets about her brother.

As I look around the table, a sense of hope settles in my chest.

Maybe I can have it all.

I watch in horror as Daniel grabs a few fries, then dunks them in his wife's milkshake. Holding a hand under the milkshake-covered fries, he feeds them to her waiting lips.

Sam and I have the same look of disbelief.

"That's disgusting," she mutters.

Daniel cradles Charlie's face, then leans down and kisses her.

"No, that's disgusting," I argue. "She has a mouth full of food."

"Not anymore," Daniel corrects, chewing what he just stole.

"I feel like we're intruding," I whisper.

"You are," he agrees, feeding his wife again.

This goes on until Charlie signals she's done.

Bored of sitting with her parents, Belle reaches for me. Although the lemon cheesecake on the table in front of me might have something to do with it.

Daniel hands Belle over the table to Samantha. With the two parents lost in their own world, Sam and I happily feed Belle spoonful of cheesecake while talking to Michael and Lara.

After Rupert is burped and both kids settled, my brothers and I stand to talk where it's a little quieter.

Seeing Sam distracted with our niece, I kiss my girl's cheek, happy when no reprimand comes.

Cold air tapers my temper, but it's not enough to cool the killer inside. "Cooper's a dead man."

We walk toward the pavement, near the empty cars.

"We need to think about this," Michael starts, ever the voice of reason.

"I'm with Kaleb."

I hold my hand out to high-five Daniel. My oldest brother stares at my hand before punching it.

"Close enough." He did agree with me, after all.

"We have the messages to Sam from his phone if he suddenly goes missing . . ." Michael doesn't need to finish his sentence.

"Fuck," I whisper-yell. "How many lives does this fucker have?"

"Michael"—Daniel sighs—"he needs to go."

Michael huffs, turning away. A smile lights up his face. Turning to the window, we see Lara feeding Charlie more milkshake-dipped fries, and Rupert resting peacefully in her arms. Sam and Belle cheer on the other side of the table like a pair of cheer-leaders.

"He needs to go," Daniel repeats, his eyes anchored to his wife.

Michael shakes his head. I have a feeling it's going to be a while before we can all agree on how to deal with the fucking cockroach.

"I just want to say thank you for today." I nod back toward the girls. "Sam was practically hyperven-tilating on the way here. I thought you'd throw at least one punch if I'm honest," I confess with a small laugh.

"Why?" Daniel frowns. "You love her?"

"I do." I nod.

"She loves you?"

I cringe. "God, I hope so."

Michael shrugs. "And we love you both."

Daniel nods like that's all the explanation needed, and I guess it is.

"So neither of you want to hit me?" I double-check.

"Should we?" Daniel frowns, turning back to his family.

"Yes!"

"Why?" Michael asks.

"Because I fucked your sister," I snap. I guess I don't fully understand their lack of disapproval after all.

Daniel stops moving, his hand held high as he returns Belle's wave.

"Politely," I rush, but both men stare blankly, "can we go back to you not wanting to punch me in the face?"

"No," Daniel says, shaking his head and taking a step toward me.

The sound of a car idling close by draws our attention. *Thank fuck!*

Seeing Cooper in the driver's seat, I curse.

Motherfucker, today is not the day.

"Kaleb," Michael warns, but it falls on deaf ears.

Cooper rolls to a stop in the parking lot, pressing his window down.

"You stopped fucking your sister long enough to eat?" he calls out.

A few people close by stop and stare.

Michael's hand lands on my chest, but it's not

enough. Daniel's hand joins Michael's when I continue to approach the beat-up car.

"Let him go. Not the time, not the place," he tells me lowly.

My chest heaves.

Never have I wanted to kill someone this much.

Not getting the response he wants, Cooper takes it up a notch.

Sticking his head out of the window, he starts to sing the chorus to "Sweet Home Alabama," turning his radio up. The music blares from his speakers.

He's lost his fucking mind! He looks demented.

Daniel moves to stand in front of me, his restraining hand no longer keeping me rooted. "He'll get his," he promises.

"Cooper, what are you doing?" Sheriff McCallister demands.

Seeing his old boss rush over from another parking lot, Cooper panics and peels off.

CHAPTER THIRTY-FIVE

Samantha

A commotion outside makes me turn my head.

My smile drops.

Michael and Daniel are holding Kaleb back while Cooper speeds off across the parking lot, his upper body out the driver's side window. He's turned back, yelling at Kaleb and my brothers.

I hear the screams of the other diners, and helpless, we're forced to watch as Riley Moore pulls away from her father and runs across the parking lot toward Shelby, who stands near the edge of the diner.

I twist Belle in my lap, pulling her to my chest so she doesn't see, but I can't find the strength to look away myself.

Everything happens so quickly.

My best friend screams, propelling herself forward. Riley hears the car and freezes in fear. Shelby reaches the small girl at the same time that the vehicle does.

My whole body flinches at the impact.

Shelby's body is sent airborne as she rolls over the hood of the car and into the windshield. Riley is barely visible tucked up so tightly in Shelby's arms.

The tires screech as Cooper hits the brakes.

Hitting the glass on her back, Shelby flies off the hood, turning before she hits the ground. Cooper throws his car in reverse and speeds off out of the lot.

I jump to my feet, pass Belle to Lara, and run out without a word.

My feet pound the pavement as I race to my best friend. Pushing through the crowd, I barely see her through blurry eyes.

Kaleb and Michael are helping Dr. Moore pry Riley from Shelby's stronghold. While Daniel runs to the end of the parking lot after the fleeing car, motioning police in the direction it went.

"It's me, Shelby," Doc sobs. "I'll take her. Let Riley go."

Shelby blinks up at him not making a sound, not even when he raises her oddly shaped wrist.

"I called an ambulance," Sheriff McCallister rushes.

"They need to be quick. She's going into shock." Doc shakes his head.

"Riley, are you hurt?" Kaleb asks.

"No," she cries.

"Are you sure, baby?" her dad checks.

The little girl clings to Michael.

Daniel waves down the ambulance, and I watch helplessly as Shelby is loaded onto a stretcher.

"Riley," Shelby mouths, unable to speak.

"She's right here. She's coming with us," Dr. Moore insists about his daughter.

"Sir, the child can't come," the paramedic argues.

"Shelby was holding her when she was struck. Riley needs looking over."

The little girl cries, refusing to let go of my brother.

"Go with them. I'll follow in the car," Kaleb urges.

I watch the man I love help load everyone into the ambulance.

We did this. This is our fault.

My heart cracks. My whole body shakes as I step back. My eyes never leave him as the crowd swallows me.

In a daze, I turn, drop to the curb, and sob.

I knew it would end, but I never could have predicted this.

What did we do?

"Baby, I have to go. Samantha!"

But Kaleb's voice and the feel of his hands on my face just make me cry harder.

"I'll get her home," Daniel tells him. "I'd go instead, but I can't leave Charlie and the kids."

"No, no. I understand. Take her to the cabin. Mom and Dad are there," Kaleb orders.

Lips press against my hair.

And just like that, he's gone, along with whatever we had.

CHAPTER THIRTY-SIX

Kaleb

I sit in the car for a few more minutes. It's been a long fucking day.

How did things get so out of control?

We'd been happy this morning, and now everything was fucked up. Shelby's in the hospital, and Sam's back to ignoring me.

Mom and Dad's car sits next to mine in the drive.

I never imagined being in front of this cabin and feeling this much dread again, but here we are. I can't stay out here forever.

When I walk in, the ground floor is dim, light spilling out from the kitchen.

I follow it like a moth to a flame.

Dad sits alone at the kitchen table.

"She told you." It's not a question. I can see it written all over his face.

"No." He shakes his head. "It's a small town. We knew before she came back."

"Where is she?"

"Upstairs. Lying with your mother, she's sobbing her heart out." His throat bobs. "Kaleb." He shakes his head, at a loss for words.

But he doesn't have to say them. I can't bear to hear them anyway.

Pulling out a chair, I sit opposite him. My whole body shakes, and I bite the bullet.

"I'd like to keep your surname. Please?" I beg, looking down at the wood beneath my shaking hands. "I can't stand the thought of taking that whore's name again," I whisper. I don't look up at Christopher as I keep talking. "I'll make sure Sam texts Helen every day. Every day," I promise with a nod. "And she'll be here every Sunday, without fail." A tear drops onto the table. "But she's not sleeping over every weekend. Maybe once a month."

Silence fills the kitchen. The stillness is interrupted by my odd sniffle. Wiping my cheek, I take a deep breath.

Now or never.

Looking up, I meet the eyes of the best man I know.

The silence eats at what is left of my soul.

Reaching out, Christopher wraps his hand around the nape of my neck. Using his grip, he pulls me closer. I don't resist. "You listen to me. You are now and always will be Kaleb Cromwell. A smart-ass, funny, energetic, loving, hardworking, cheeky little shit. My youngest son. A Cromwell."

My chin trembles at his words.

"The day you changed your surname sits up there as one of the best days of my life, sharing a spot with the day we adopted your brothers and the day your sis—" Dad cuts himself off, pausing before he corrects his words. "The day that Samantha was born and the day you moved in. Topped only by the day I married your mother. You will always be welcome in this house, Kaleb, because you're family. My son," he says, stressing the last two words.

I'm openly crying. Dad leans forward, resting his forehead on mine.

"My son," he repeats in a whisper. "My favorite." He smirks.

I laugh at his words, snotty and breathy. We all know Samantha is his favorite, a spot earned by being the only girl. But I don't voice that.

Dad gives his own sniffle, pulling back. "Don't break her heart, Kaleb," he pleads.

"I won't," I promise, shaking my head. "I'm going to marry her," I vow, looking him in the eye. "I'll always take care of her."

"You have been for a while," Dad acknowledges. "I just never imagined it was because of this." He waves his arm vaguely, but we both know what he means.

"It wasn't always." I shake my head. "The past few years, our relationship has been . . ." I shrug because the man needs to hear about me falling in love with his daughter about as much as I want to talk about it.

Dad cringes but motions upstairs. "The longer you leave her, the worse it'll be. Go talk to her."

I push back from the table and stand.

"And Kaleb," Dad calls.

I wait at the bottom of the stairs, my heart beat picking up. "Don't let Helen hear you calling her by her first name. It'll crush her heart. We're your mom and dad. We love you no matter what."

I nod, my chest expanding as the vise gripping my heart finally releases.

"I love you, too, Dad."

I knock lightly on my parents' door. It kills me to wait, but Mom opens the door a few seconds later.

"Hi."

Lame, Kaleb.

I wait with bated breath. Will Mom react the same as Dad?

Soft lavender perfume surrounds me as I'm pulled into a deep hug.

"Have you spoken to your dad?"

Quickly wiping away tears, I nod.

"Good." She smiles, and her fingers join mine in drying my face.

"Are you going to make this right? I don't like seeing any of my kids cry, never mind two."

"Yes, ma'am," I promise.

"Any news on Shelby?"

I shake my head. "We're going to the hospital once I fix this."

Mom nods. "I'll be downstairs with your dad."

I wait for her to leave before closing the door and approaching the bed.

"Don't," Sam yells the minute my hand touches her back.

I ignore it as she tries to shrug me off. I rub her back until her breathing settles.

"Shelby and Riley?" she asks, her voice muffled in the pillow.

"Riley is perfect, not a scratch on her. Shelby . . . is alive. I don't know the extent of her injuries. I wanted to get back to you."

I lean down and press a kiss to her covered shoulder.

"Don't," she snaps, rolling onto her back. "We did this."

"Kyle Cooper did this," I correct gently.

"While trying to get at us."

"Sammy," I start softly.

"Don't Sammy me, Kaleb," she huffs. Propelling forward, she shoves at my chest with all she has.

"Samantha," I warn.

"We did this, Kaleb. We did," she cries, hitting my arm and then her chest over and over. "We did. I did."

"Careful," I reprimand, catching her arm. "I don't want you to hurt yourself."

Samantha struggles in my hold, wriggling to her knees for more leverage.

I back away, standing from the bed.

Something flashes across her face.

"Or is that what you need?"

Sam's eyes meet mine.

"You want to hurt." It's not a question. She needs a release, but she can't voice it. "Fine." I nod.

Reaching back, I pull my T-shirt over my head.

"What the fuck are you doing?" she hisses.

"Giving us both what we need." My hands drop to my pants. "You need to feel something, and I need you. Besides, a good orgasm will do you good."

"Not happening."

I tackle her to the bed before she finishes. Sam struggles below me, hitting my chest and arms, but she avoids my face.

She wants to hit me; she doesn't want to hurt me.

"Tell me to stop," I challenge, catching her arms.

"Get the fuck off me."

"Tell me to stop," I repeat, kneeling above her so that I can roll her onto her stomach with her arms captured in the middle of her back.

"I hate you."

"Tell me to stop," I whisper, moving her onto her knees.

I unbutton and shove down her pants, taking her panties with them.

Releasing her arms, I push her forward, forcing her hands to catch her.

"Tell me to stop," I say one last time as I shuck down my pants.

No?

Hands on her waist, I give her zero warning before burying my cock inside her. One strong thrust and my hips meet her ass.

"Ahhhh," Sam cries out.

Pulling out, I bottom back in, her hips shooting back to meet me.

Our hips meet in a clash of frustration.

Fuck me. I will never get enough of her.

Over and over, Sam sends her body back to accept mine. My left hand grabs her tit. Shoving her bra out of the way, I grip her hard enough to leave bruises. My right hand locks in her hair, tugging her back harder than before. Her scalp must be screaming.

She wants pain, I'll give her pain.

Wetness builds between her legs, and her pussy ripples as she nears the edge quickly. Pinching her nipple, I twist and pull, ripping the orgasm from her.

She's loud and frantic as she comes, coating my cock with her juices.

I push through her tensing muscles, giving no reprieve.

Sam cries out again as her cunt contracts once more.

Over and over, I fuck her as hard as I can. Each cry of pain is followed by an orgasm bigger than the last. The headboard knocks against the wall with the force that I thrust.

Finally, her continued denials turn to begging.

"Please, please."

"Give me one more," I order.

Releasing her chest, I bring my hand down on her ass. Every time I pull out, my hand rains down in the space between us.

The ache in my hand adds to the ache in my balls. I need to come. I need to fill her. Remind her who I am. What we are.

Roaring, I grip both of her shoulders and yank her back onto my hips. Thrusting and pulling with everything I have.

I know it hurts her. My own hips feel sore, but I know it's the right thing to do when she screams in pleasure.

Her orgasm shakes her entire body. Our juices mix and flow out of her, and she gushes with every pump.

Together, we're left breathless. My shaking legs are barely able to hold me as I climb off the bed.

"I get why you like sleeping in here. The bed's comfy." I wink, buckling my pants.

CHAPTER THIRTY-SEVEN

Samantha

My face pales. "What are we doing?" I ask, climbing off the bed. I close my eyes when I feel cum rush out of me. It drips down my thighs, and the feel of him leaving me as my body cools is a slap in the face.

"Us." He smooths my hair back. "We're just being us."

My tears win, spilling over my lashes.

"Are we really going to rip our family apart for something we can't even say aloud?"

Kaleb rears back as if I slapped him.

"I'm not ashamed of us, Sam. I told you before that I was done fighting this, and now so are you. This is happening, Samantha. If you need me to make that decision for you, if your morals won't allow you to accept us, then fine, I'll do that. I'll be that force for you," he tells me with a small nod. His hands reach up and cradle my face. "You and I are happening." His thumb wipes away a tear on my cheek. "I'm going to fuck you." His nose nudges mine. "I'm going to provide for you." He kisses my right cheek. "I'm going to punish you." He kisses my left cheek. "I'm going to love you," he whispers, his lips brushing mine. "And when you're ready, I'm going to marry you."

"We shouldn't." I shake my head. "We can't."

We stand there together in the middle of our parents' bedroom, our lips barely touching, the smell of sex pungent.

"I love you, Samantha Cromwell," Kaleb declares. Gray eyes pierce into mine. "And you," he breathes, "you're going to let me. I'm not asking if that's what you need, but I'd rather you choose."

I cry as he pulls me closer.

"You own me, Samantha. I'm yours."

Our lips clash, his teeth nip before his tongue soothes the pain. Together, we fight for dominance until finally I relent. My arms wind around his shoulders, and my hand cradles the back of his head.

He and I are wrong. Everything about this is wrong, yet at this moment, my life has never felt more right.

I love Kaleb Cromwell, and anyone who has a problem with that can take it up with him.

"I love you, too."

A devilish smile takes over his face. "That's my girl."

CHAPTER THIRTY-EIGHT

Kaleb

I glance over at a silent Samantha.

Red-eyed and pale, she looks tired and older than her twenty-two years under the fluorescent lights of the hospital elevator.

Hearing the ding, I reach out and take her hand, happy when she doesn't pull away.

"Come on, baby," I encourage, leading her down the corridor toward her best friend's room.

The night nurse looks up as we pass but doesn't comment on our late visit.

Money will do that for you.

The blinds are open in Shelby's room. Through the slats, I see Leonard stand.

Quietly, he joins us in the hall.

"How is she?" I ask.

He shakes his head and blinks.

"Awake. On good pain meds." He manages to get out.

Samantha isn't the only one with red eyes.

"Riley?" he asks.

"She's perfect. More than happy to be having a sleepover with her new aunt Lara and uncle Michael," I reassure.

He runs a hand through his hair. "I can't thank you enough."

"Shelby's family. That makes you family?" I state. Raising a brow, I dare him to argue.

"She could use some of that right now." He nods back into the room. Pinching the bridge of his nose, we watch as he tries to calm himself. "She was pregnant."

I stand straighter at his words.

Was.

Sam doesn't wait to hear anymore. Slipping her hand from mine, she rushes into her friend's room.

We watch as my girl slips off her sneakers and crawls onto the bed. Sam wraps her body around Shelby, careful of the sling and bandages.

That's all it takes. The young brunette breaks down, and her sobs claw at my chest.

"How far along?" I ask, meeting his eyes.

"Only a few weeks." Removing his glasses, he wipes his own eyes. "We didn't know."

My heart breaks at the pain coming from the

room and the man before me. Placing a hand on his shoulder, I offer the only words I can. "I'm sorry."

Leonard and I join the girls in the hospital room.

Hearing us enter, Shelby turns her face into the pillow away from us.

Sam follows suit, moving with her. Spooning her friend, Samantha strokes Shelby's hair, whispering words lost in the little space separating them.

Leaning over the bottom of the bed, I reach out to grasp Shelby's foot. "I'm sorry, sweet girl."

My words are drowned out by her tears, but I feel her foot flex under my fingers.

The room slowly stills, Shelby falling into a light sleep.

Leonard shifts on the small sofa that he and I sit on. "She has a broken clavicle where the car impacted and a dislocated shoulder."

I eye the sling on her right arm.

"Bruising along the entire right side of her body. She's lucky her hip wasn't broken, but she'll feel it when she walks for a few weeks."

I swallow, keeping my eyes on the bed.

"A broken wrist where she tried to break their fall."

Her left wrist lays near the edge of the bed, the plaster bright pink.

"It's Riley's favorite color. She thought it would be less scary. The doctor says her headache will ease, but we need to be wary of the concussion."

Grief fills me.

"This is your fault."

Closing my eyes, I feel my tears break free at his words. Sam's doubts from earlier attack me.

No!

"He may have been there because of us, but Cooper's actions are his own," I push back.

"I'm not talking about the car plowing into my family." He shakes his head, giving an empty laugh. "You and your brothers should have taken care of him well before now. He shouldn't still be on this earth to be driving!" Leonard hisses.

My head snaps around.

He glares at me through his black-rimmed glasses.

"You've been fucking around with him for years. This"—he points at the bed—"is on the three of you."

My heart thumps in my throat. What does he know?

"Before now, I didn't give a fuck what you did, none of you. You kept it to yourselves, but this . . ." He looks away.

"We'll take care of it," I say carefully.

"No, you had your chance."

Interesting. It seems my family isn't the only ones with a secret.

"Shelby's family." I repeat my words from earlier.

Silence fills the room.

"Then maybe it needs to be a family event," he relents.

We sit, watching our girls.

I'm not worried that he knows. He clearly has skeletons of his own. Ones we should probably dig up for safekeeping.

I promised Samantha that I would make this right, and that's exactly what I'm going to do.

My eyes find my girl.

My life.

My strength.

Nothing and no one will ever take her again.

EPILOGUE

Kaleb

Jogging down the last few steps to the ground floor of the cabin, I pause.

Mom and Sam are plating up the last of the food to take outside.

"Finally!" Mom huffs playfully. "Where did you run off to?"

"I just needed to go fetch something," I say evasively. My left hand drops to pat the pocket of my slacks, and my heart races as if they can see through the material. "What, a man can't have a free moment around here?"

"A man probably could." My girl smirks.

A smile lights up my face.

"Behave, you two. Baby, grab the deviled eggs on

your way out, please," Mom asks, looking at me. "You okay with the salad and tongs?"

"I got it," Sam reassures.

As soon as Mom is out the door, I trap my girl against the kitchen island. "That wasn't very nice," I pout.

Sam laughs, wrapping her arms around my neck. "You like me when I'm not nice."

My hands slide around her waist, settling on the curve of her ass. "I like you naughty. There's a difference."

She smiles against my lips. "I'll make it up to you."

"Hmmm," I hum. Stepping back, I take in her blue sundress. "Have I told you how beautiful you look today?"

"You did." She nods. "Several times but I could hear it again."

I slant my lips over hers. "Fucking gorgeous."

"Remind me why we're dressed nicely for a family barbecue."

"I wanted everyone to look nice for my birthday, and you love me."

My kisses move down the side of her neck. The taste of sunscreen mixes with her unique taste.

"Don't leave a mark," she warns.

"Hey, you two lovebirds, knock it off. Shelby just pulled up," Michael's voice booms.

I pull back with a groan. "Remind me to tell Lara that it was Michael who broke her Christmas bauble."

"The glass one?" Sam gasps.

"Yeah." I release her, making my way around the counter to pick up the platter of eggs. "He knocked it off the tree on accident. He's commissioned another one from some place in Maine."

Sam pauses in picking up the salad. "She thinks Rex did it."

"I know." I chuckle, following her out.

As if he heard his name, the golden retriever joins us at the kitchen door. Tripping, he misses a step with his back leg. All energy and no grace. *Takes after his dad.* I laugh.

Seeing her baby get underfoot, Lara calls out to him.

"Rexy!"

The eager pup sprints away.

I take a second to watch my family.

My family. Two words I never thought I'd get to say.

People who taught me what unconditional love truly feels like.

My heart swells.

Reaching down, I pat the small square box in my pocket again.

Best Fourth of July ever.

The End.

ABOUT THE AUTHOR

Jennifer Ivy is an author that loves to write dark romance.

The author can be found on several social media sites, such as:

Instagram; jenniferivy_author
TikTok; jennifer_author
Goodreads; Jennifer Ivy

ALSO BY JENNIFER IVY

A Killer's Love Series

Mine

Claim

Taken

Blood

Lock